GYPSY MAGIC

As the King spoke, there was a sudden depth in his voice, and Laetitia thought there was a fire in his eyes that had not been there before. She would have taken a step away, but his arms went round her.

Before she could even put up her hands, his lips came down on hers. Even as she thought she must struggle and be free of him there was a strange magic. It seemed to grow and intensify until she felt not only her lips grow soft and yielding, but her whole body move as if to music.

He took his lips from hers to say:

"I want you, now at this moment, as I know you want me!"

Then the King was kissing her again, but not now on her lips. Instead his mouth moved over the softness of her neck, and it gave Laetitia a sensation she had never known before, which made her quiver against him, her breath coming quickly from between her lips.

"I . . . love . . . you!" she whispered. "I love . . . you . . . love you!"

Bantam Books by Barbara Cartland
Ask your bookseller for the books you have missed

Barbara Cartland's Library of Love Series

Gypsy Magic

Barbara Cartland

BANTAM BOOKS
TORONTO · NEW YORK · LONDON · SYDNEY

GYPSY MAGIC

A Bantam Book / May 1983

ISBN 0-553-23285-1

Published simultaneously in the United States and Canada

Bantam Books are published by Bantam Books, Inc. Its trademark,
consisting of the words "Bantam Books" and the portrayal of a rooster
is Registered in U.S. Patent and Trademark Office and in other
countries. Marca Registrada. Bantam Books, Inc., 666 Fifth Avenue,
New York, New York 10103.

PRINTED IN THE UNITED STATES OF AMERICA

H   0 9 8 7 6 5 4 3 2 1

Author's Note

I became interested in Gypsies in 1960 when I found they were unjustly treated in being moved every twenty-four hours, so it was impossible for Gypsy children to go to school. After a bitter battle which took three years, I eventually got the law altered so that Local Authorities were obliged to provide Camps for their own Gypsies.

Now in Hertfordshire there are eight County Council Camps, and my own, which is, I believe, the only entirely Romany Gypsy Camp in the world and which the Gypsies themselves christened "Barbaraville."

I have learnt in my dealings with the Romany Gypsies how extremely moral they are and how they marry for life.

Romany Gypsies are very secretive about their beliefs, customs, and even their language, so that the little which has been written about them is often untrue.

They have suffered terrible persecutions in every country in Europe. Beginning in 1939, Germany started their internment with the aim of their entire extinction. More than 400,000 Gypsies lost their lives under the Nazis before the end of the Second World War.

Today, most countries are following our lead and trying to find some way in which the Gypsy children can be educated.

The Kalderash Gypsies believe they are the only authentic Gypsies. They came from the Balkans, then from Central Europe, and are divided into five groups:

1. LOVARI, in France, called Hungarians.
2. BOYHAS, who come from Transylvania.
3. LURI (or LULT), the Indian tribe.
4. TSCHURARI (TSCHURARI, CHRUAI), who live apart from the other Kaldarash Gypsies.
5. TURCO-AMERICANS, who emigrated from Turkey to the United States before returning to Europe.

Chapter One

1825

"It is no use," Princess Laetitia said to her sister, "I shall never get this gown to look anything but dowdy."

"You will look lovely in it whatever it is like," Princess Marie-Henriette replied.

Laetitia smiled.

"You know perfectly well that whatever we wear will be wrong when Cousin Augustina sees it."

Marie-Henriette laughed.

"She is afraid that we might receive even one compliment that she thinks ought to be paid to Stephanie! Anyway, she dislikes us all, Mama included."

Laetitia looked quickly at the door, as if she was afraid her mother might overhear. Then she said in a lower voice:

"I know, Hettie, but do not say so. You know it upsets Mama, and she has been very depressed lately."

"It is not surprising," Marie-Henriette replied. "With no money and what one might call the 'hostilities' coming from the Palace all the time, I only wish we could go somewhere else."

"There is no answer to that," Laetitia replied, "so we just have to put up with it."

As she spoke she laid down the gown she was trying to

1

alter and walked to the window to look out onto the courtyard.

Just a short distance from the Palace were a number of small, attractive houses centred round a courtyard.

They were the Grace and Favour Houses which were allotted to the Grand Duke's relatives and to Statesmen who had served their country and who were too poor to afford a house of their own.

When Prince Paul of Ovenstadt was killed fighting with his Regiment against an invading Army of another country, which was quickly repelled, his family had to leave their home, an attractive house in which they had lived in comfort, and move into a small and rather cramped Grace and Favour House, for which they were, however, very grateful.

But what the two Princesses and their brother, when he was not with his Regiment, minded was what Marie-Henriette had called the "hostilities" coming from the Palace.

This was due not to the Grand Duke, who had been extremely fond of his cousin Prince Paul, but to the Grand Duchess.

Since the Grand Duke Louis had had an elder brother he had not expected to inherit the throne, and he and Prince Paul were brought up together and had always sworn they would never marry.

However, what happened was that first Prince Paul fell head-over-heels in love with the very beautiful daughter of a nobleman with Royal blood in his veins who lived on the other side of the country.

Because the Prince was a comparatively unimportant member of the hierarchy, after some feeble opposition he was allowed to marry the girl of his choice, the only real protests coming from his cousin Louis, who felt companionless and alone for the first time in his life.

Six months later, Louis's elder brother died of a fever which the Doctors could not diagnose, and as soon as Louis became the Crown Prince, pressure was brought on him to marry.

Unfortunately, because he was a charming and courteous man, he was pressurised into taking as his wife a Prussian Princess who undoubtedly brought some benefits to the country over which she was to reign, but she immediately became the dominating partner of their marriage.

As the years passed and she became the Grand Duchess, she asserted her authority to the point where there were numerous jokes both inside and outside Ovenstadt as to "who wore the trousers."

They had two children—a son, Otto, who was spoilt from the moment he was born and became almost as obnoxious as his mother, and a daughter, Stephanie, who was exactly like her father and therefore loved by everybody who knew her.

Because the Grand Duchess had to have everything her own way and was possessive, acquisitive, and extremely jealous, she disliked not only Prince Paul's lovely wife, Olga, but also her children.

This was not surprising when it was obvious to everybody that Laetitia and Marie-Henriette were becoming more and more beautiful every day.

What was more, their brother, Prince Kyril, was immeasurably better-looking, more intelligent, and certainly a better sportsman than the Crown Prince Otto.

The girls in the Grace and Favour House were snubbed by the Grand Duchess on every possible occasion, and she made it palpably clear that they were not welcome at the Palace.

She had to invite them on State occasions simply because their father, Prince Paul, had been so popular with the Statesmen and the officials and the people of Ovenstadt that she dare not leave them out.

But, as Laetitia often said, she would have done so if she could.

However, when the two girls were alone, they often wondered what would become of them in the future.

"One thing that is quite obvious," Laetitia said a dozen times, "is that there is no chance of anybody finding husbands for us until Stephanie has one!"

She paused and went on reflectively:

"Even then I think Cousin Augustina will make every excuse to keep us out of sight of any eligible bachelors, unless of course there is a chance of one taking us away from Ovenstadt forever."

Laetitia did not talk bitterly but merely as if she was stating a fact.

She usually found it easier to laugh than to cry about it.

At the same time, now that she was eighteen she resented that there was not enough money to have pretty gowns for herself and Marie-Henriette, who was sixteen months younger, and her mother had to scrimp and pinch even to feed them properly.

"How angry it would make Papa!" she would say when they were deliberately excluded from some party at the Palace to which they should have been invited!

She said the same when it was impossible to make the very little money they had go any further and they were unable to offer hospitality to those who invited them to their homes.

Her mother had sighed the last time she had said it to her.

"I know, darling, but I suppose it is a cross we have to bear."

"I cannot think why," Laetitia replied argumenta- tively. "Papa died for his country, and apparently we, quite unjustly, are being punished for it."

For a moment Princess Olga sat thinking. Then she said:

"I know it is tiresome for you, darling, but at the same time, I would not wish to live in the Palace, however comfortable it might be."

Both Laetitia and Marie-Henriette gave little screams of protest.

Then they were all laughing.

"Can you imagine what it would be like," Laetitia asked, "with Cousin Augustina coming down to breakfast and starting by telling us we were too early or too late, our hair was untidy, our gowns were incorrectly buttoned, and, what was more, our faces were all wrong?"

"Whatever we do is wrong to her," Marie-Henriette agreed.

"That is enough, girls!" Princess Olga interrupted. "Whatever we feel about Cousin Augustina, Cousin Louis is very fond of us."

"That is true," Laetitia said. "At the same time, he is too weak to do anything about the way his wife behaves. What a pity it is that Papa's father did not come to the throne!"

"I suppose second sons since the beginning of time have always complained at not being the eldest," Princess Olga replied, "but Papa did not mind. He did not wish to be the Grand Duke. He just wanted to enjoy life and to be happy with all of us."

The Princess always looked sad as she spoke of her husband, and now on her lovely face there was an expression which made the girls hastily start talking of something else.

They adored their mother, and it seemed a perverse cruelty on the part of fate that their father should have been killed when he was so happily married, while his cousin Louis was stuck forever with a woman whom, if the truth was known, he actively disliked.

The Grand Duke had therefore withdrawn from a great deal of public life, leaving the Grand Duchess to make decisions for him and to receive Statesmen on his behalf, and she deliberately pushed him more and more into the background.

Sometimes when it seemed as if he could bear it no longer he would call at the Grace and Favour House to see Princess Olga.

He would sit in the small Sitting-Room which was so unlike the huge Salons of the Palace, telling her of his troubles.

"I know how much you miss Paul," he had said the last time he called, "and I too find myself missing him more every day. If he were here, I know that he would help me and prevent me from being so ineffective."

"You must not talk like that, Louis!" Princess Olga had said in her soft voice. "The people love you."

"When they get a chance to see me," the Grand Duke replied, "and I know I am blamed for a lot of laws that were not of my making."

He paused before he said:

"I suppose you are aware, as everybody else is, that the new Prime Minister is in Augustina's pocket?"

Princess Olga did not reply. She merely inclined her head, and the Grand Duke went on:

"He calls on her every day and does not pay me the courtesy of even pretending to consult me. He shows the State papers first of all to my wife, and then when they have decided what to do they ask me for my signature on them."

"Why do you not refuse?" Princess Olga enquired.

"Because I am not man enough to stand up to a scene," the Grand Duke answered, "and that is where I miss Paul. He always fought my battles for me, and without him I am like a man who has lost the use of his right arm. I feel it is not worth making the effort alone and unsupported."

Princess Olga sighed, then she reached out and put her hand on his.

"I think, Louis dear, you should try."

"To do what?" he asked. "You know as well as I do that Augustina has taken everything into her own hands. It is she who rules the country, and if I rebelled against her decisions I should doubtless soon find myself certified as a lunatic or imprisoned in one of the dungeons!"

They both laughed.

At the same time, there was, Princess Olga thought sadly, a great deal of truth in what the Grand Duke was saying.

She was quite sure that the Grand Duchess would be utterly ruthless if anybody tried to topple her from the seat of power.

When the Grand Duke had left, she had merely prayed that somehow by some miracle he would be saved from what she realised was a life of misery which was almost approaching despair.

Sometimes she thought of appealing to him on behalf of the girls and suggesting that now that Laetitia was

eighteen, a Ball should be given for her at the Palace,
which would give her a chance to meet eligible young
Princes from neighbouring countries or at least some of the
noble families whom the Grand Duchess seldom invited to
the Court.

But she knew that even if the Grand Duke agreed, his
wife would be violently opposed to the idea and he would
not have the strength to insist on the Ball being given.

When she had told Laetitia what she thought, her
daughter had said:

"You are quite right, Mama. I am certain Cousin Louis
would be overruled and nothing would be done. At the
same time, sooner or later somebody will have to stand up
to her, although it cannot be you."

"If only your father were here," Princess Olga had said
with a sigh.

Then they were both aware that the conversation had
gone full circle and nothing would be done about it.

Now, standing at the window, Laetitia said with her
back to her sister:

"I think that rather than being faint-hearted because
we cannot get the things we want, we should perhaps try
witchcraft!"

"Witchcraft?" Marie-Henriette exclaimed. "We do not
know any witches."

"Gypsies can do magic," Laetitia replied.

"They have little chance to do it here," Marie-
Henriette said. "You know Cousin Augustina has banned
them from the Capital and told them to keep to the fields
and mountains unless they wish to be expelled altogether
from Ovenstadt."

"That is the kind of thing she would do!" Laetitia
answered. "It will only make the people hate her more than
they do already. After all, there is Gypsy blood in a great
number of Ovenstadts, including us."

Marie-Henriette laughed.

"You had better not let Cousin Augustina hear you talk
about Gypsy blood, or you will be sent away in case you
contaminate her!"

"I have always been told that Prussians hate Gypsies,"

Laetitia said reflectively, "but to us they are part of our life, and the country would not be the same without them."

As she spoke she was thinking of the colourful bands of Gypsies who roamed in the valleys and of their music, which always stirred her heart whenever she heard it and made her long to start dancing.

Her father had told her how when he was young he and his cousin Louis would often join the Gypsies round their camp-fires and listen to the glorious, wild melodies they played on their violins.

They would also watch the young Gypsy girls dancing with a grace that was characteristic of their race.

"It is a grace you possess yourself, my darling," he had said to Laetitia when she was thirteen.

"How exciting, Papa! Are you quite sure I have it?"

"Quite sure," her father had answered. "Just as I am sure that when you grow older you will be very beautiful and I shall be very proud of you!"

Stories of Gypsy life had always intrigued Laetitia, even though she knew it was something she dare not mention at the Palace.

There was a tale that far back in the history of the family, their great-great-great-grandfather who was Grand Duke married twice but there were no children of either marriage.

His second wife was very much younger than he was, and as he grew older he became frantic to have an heir.

If he did not do so, the succession would pass from the family of Rákónzi, to which they all belonged, to a family they all disliked and which had over the years become lazy, debauched, and in consequence most unsuited to rule.

The Grand Duke had therefore taken his wife to Physicians all over Europe and to Healing Spas, and finally as a last resort he had sought the help of the Gypsies.

The legend which was afterwards always told in whispers recounted that because the Grand Duke was unwell at the time, the Grand Duchess had gone alone to the camp of the most important tribe in the whole country.

She had been welcomed by their *Voivode*, or King, who was young, dark, and very handsome.

She had taken part in a feast at which the Gypsies filled their most prized possession of jewelled goblets with the rarest wine the vineyards could produce.

After they had feasted there had been music and dancing round the camp-fire.

Very late, when the violins were still playing but a number of the older Gypsies had fallen asleep, the King had taken the Grand Duchess away into the woods.

There under the stars he had used on her the magic which would ensure an heir to the throne.

It was a very romantic story, and Prince Paul had finished by saying:

"The majority of Rákónzis are red-headed and fair-skinned, but occasionally one of us is born with dark hair, dark eyes, and fair skin like yours, my precious."

Laetitia had given a little cry of delight.

"And that, Papa, is the magic the Gypsies gave the Grand Duchess!"

"Look in the mirror," her father said, "and you will see that your hair has the blue lights that all brunettes long to have."

He smiled affectionately as he went on:

"While your lashes are also dark, my dearest, your eyes are as green as the Steppes over which the Gypsies roam, and your white skin, which feels like a magnolia petal, is an inheritance of my family and your mother's."

It was true, Laetitia found when she thought about herself, that she did look different from the other members of the Rákónzi family.

She had really never thought about it before and had taken it for granted that she should be a brunette while Marie-Henriette was a blonde like her mother.

But while her mother's hair was as golden as the sunshine, there was something in the darkness of her eyes that was not quite as one would have expected.

Laetitia thought there was some small characteristic of the Gypsies to be found in the Grand Duke.

The story was to all three of Prince Paul's children very exciting and romantic, but when the Grand Duchess assumed power she would not have it mentioned.

"Legends of that sort," she remarked firmly, "are always lies thought up by primitive, uncivilised people because they have nothing else to think about."

She paused to say more positively:

"I have gone carefully into the family-tree, and I assure you there is not one word of truth in the story that there is Gypsy blood in the Rákónzis."

She waited to see if anybody contradicted her, but they thought it wiser not to do so, and she continued:

"I have even found in the history of the family that the Grand Duchess who was responsible for all this nonsense was treated by a very able Physician in France, which ensured her having a child who later became the Grand Duke."

She paused before she added finally:

"So that tale is not to be repeated again by anybody in this family!"

Laetitia said nothing, but when she returned home she looked at herself in the mirror and knew that her hair was different from that of other girls who were simply dark instead of being fair.

She remembered too how her father had said that her gracefulness came from the Gypsies.

When she was alone she would dance, and she had found that her body was supple enough to make the turns, the twists, and the double-jointed movements of the Gypsies.

She could also spring as they could do into the air and leap over a lighted fire, appearing almost as if she flew from the ground in a magical way of their own.

Because she was determined to know more about the life of the Gypsies, whenever she was out riding away from the Palace, and therefore felt free of her cousin's restrictions, she would stop and talk to any of the tribes she met as they wandered through the flower-filled valleys or climbed up the sides of the mountains.

Because they knew who she was and felt honoured by her presence, they would not only talk to her and answer some of the questions she asked, but they also taught her some of their Romany words.

Because she had a retentive memory, she soon had quite a large vocabulary.

She found, as she had expected, that they knew the legend of the Rákónzi Gypsy ancestor and that they admired her dark hair because they believed, as she did, that it was inherited from them.

Because the Grand Duchess hated the Gypsies, this last year she had taken to persecuting them whenever she got the chance.

She banished them farther and farther away from the Capital, so that Laetitia found it more difficult to locate them as she had been able to do in the past.

"How can Cousin Augustina be so cruel?" she had asked her mother angrily when it was reported in the newspapers that two Gypsies accused of crimes of which they swore their innocence had been executed.

"It will create a great deal of ill feeling," Princess Olga said with a sigh. "Our Gypsies have always been kind and friendly and part of our country."

"You must speak with Cousin Louis, Mama, and beg him to do something about it," Laetitia said.

"I will try," her mother replied, "but you know, dearest, that he finds it very hard to do anything without the support of the Prime Minister."

"Who does what Cousin Augustina tells him!" Laetitia finished. "Oh, Mama, she is a horrible woman! I only hope the Gypsies put a spell on her to make her suffer as much as she makes them suffer!"

Princess Olga gave a little cry of protest.

"Do not talk like that, dearest. It is unlucky!"

"Why should it be unlucky for us when we love the Gypsies?" Laetitia asked. "Papa said I have inherited my hair from the Gypsies and the way I move, and I am very proud of it."

Princess Olga smiled, but she knew it was not only because Laetitia was so beautiful but also because she was a constant reminder of the Gypsy blood in the Rákónzi family that the Grand Duchess took every opportunity of humiliating her by excluding her from the parties she gave at the

Palace, to which she should have been invited because of her rank.

As they were so poor and could hardly afford to entertain at all themselves, Princess Olga wondered again and again what she could do about it.

She had prayed night after night that she would have help in some way or another, first for her beloved son, who was finding it hard in his Regiment to live on the very small allowance she was able to give him; secondly for Laetitia, who at eighteen should be enjoying far more of a social life; and lastly for Marie-Henriette, who in her own way was growing to be as beautiful as her sister.

"Oh, Paul, Paul!" the Princess cried in the darkness. "Help me to do what I can for the children. At the moment I seem to be up against a blank wall!"

As always when she thought of her husband, she felt her whole body reaching out to him, longing for him to be near her.

However, she knew it was a mistake to display her sorrow to her children.

It was therefore only when she was alone with the Grand Duke that she talked of Paul, because he had loved him as she had and it did not matter if he saw her tears.

Still standing at the window, Laetitia said:

"I am going to do a Gypsy spell, or rather make a wish that something will happen."

"What do you want to happen?" asked Marie-Henriette, who was still sitting at the table sewing.

"Anything," Laetitia replied. "Sometimes I feel as if we are incarcerated here and gradually we shall just grow older and older and this will be our grave."

"Do not talk like that!" Marie-Henriette exclaimed. "It makes me feel creepy."

"A Gypsy to whom I talked told me of a spell which, if you believe it strongly enough, will always make your wish come true."

"Well, do it!" Marie-Henriette said. "I cannot think what you are waiting for."

"He told me you have to do it under a full moon," Laetitia said, "which is not for another week. If I am going to have a magic wish, it might as well be a good one, so think of all the things you want, Hettie, and I will make a mental parcel of them."

Marie-Henriette laughed.

"My wishes would fill a trunk! You can start off with a dozen new gowns, and at least three or four Balls at which to wear them."

"Very well," Laetitia said. "I will put that on the list. Anything else?"

"A tall, handsome, rich Prince, who will dance with me and pay for the gowns."

Laetitia laughed.

"That would be extremely improper!"

"Well, it is unlikely that Mama would be able to pay for them."

"But she will, because that is one of my wishes," Laetitia argued. "And if you want a tall, handsome Prince, I want one too!"

"Then it is quite easy," Marie-Henriette said. "You must wish for a pair of Princes who are both tall, handsome, and immensely rich, and of course unmarried."

Laetitia laughed.

"I think what we are asking for is as likely as finding ourselves flying to the moon, but the Gypsies believe their magic never fails."

She gave a sudden exclamation.

"Good Heavens! It cannot be! But it is!"

"What is it?"

"It is Stephanie. She is running here, and she is alone!"

"I do not believe it!" Marie-Henriette said. "You know as well as I do that she is never allowed to move without that grumpy old Baroness in attendance."

"She is alone!"

Laetitia turned from the window to run across the room and into the small Hall, and Marie-Henriette heard her open the door.

"Stephanie! What a surprise!" she cried.

Then as Princess Stephanie came into the Hall, Laetitia saw that she was crying.

"What has happened? What is the matter?"

"Oh, Laetitia . . . I had to . . . see you!" Stephanie answered.

"But of course," Laetitia said. "Come into the Sitting-Room. Mama is resting, so only Hettie and I are here."

The Princess moved into the small Sitting-Room, and Marie-Henriette got up from the table to kiss her.

"It is lovely to see you, Stephanie," she said. "It seems ages since you have been to see us."

"I know . . . I know," Stephanie replied, the tears running down her face, "but Mama would . . . not let me come . . . and now I have . . . run away when that ghastly old Baroness was not . . . looking."

She gave a little sob and said:

"I escaped through a . . . side-door and ran . . . all the way . . . here."

Laetitia helped her into a chair.

"Sit down, dearest," she said. "Take off your bonnet and tell us what has upset you."

Stephanie had come without a handkerchief and Marie-Henriette gave her one.

She wiped her eyes, but that seemed to make her cry more than she was already, the tears running down her small, pointed face.

She was very pretty, with golden hair with touches of red in it and the hazel-gold eyes which were characteristic of the Rákónzis.

She bore no resemblance to her mother, who had strong, hard Prussian features, and it was easy to see that she was her father's daughter. Actually, she and Marie-Henriette were very much alike.

When Stephanie had taken off her bonnet, Laetitia went down on her knees beside the chair and put her arms round her.

"Tell us, dearest, what has upset you," she said. "I cannot bear you to cry like that."

"Oh . . . Laetitia! All I want to . . . do is to . . . die!"

"You must not say such things," Laetitia said. "What could have happened to make you so unhappy?"

For a moment it seemed as if the Princess was unable

to speak, then almost incoherently the words burst from her.

"Mama has . . . told me I am to . . . marry King . . . Viktor!"

Laetitia stared at her.

"King Viktor of Zvotana?"

"Y-yes."

The monosyllable brought another burst of crying, then Stephanie said:

"How can I possibly . . . marry him when you . . . know that I . . . love Kyril . . . and he . . . loves me?"

Both Laetitia and her sister stared at Stephanie in astonishment.

They were both aware that when Kyril was at home he and Stephanie always rode together, and that he spent a lot of time at the Palace because he said there was far more to do there than there was with them.

They had always known he was very fond of Stephanie, just as they were, but it had never crossed their minds that there was anything more between them.

"He loves me . . . he loves . . . me," Stephanie sobbed now, "and I love him! If I cannot . . . marry him I swear . . . I will . . . kill myself!"

Laetitia made a little cry of protest and held Stephanie closer as she said:

"You must not say such wicked things! Have you told your mother how you feel about him?"

"No, of course . . . not!" Stephanie replied. "Mama would be . . . furious! She is very . . . ambitious for . . . me."

Both sisters knew this was true, and Laetitia was aware that there was nothing the Grand Duchess would enjoy more than having a close alliance with a more prosperous country than Ovenstadt and for Stephanie to be a Queen.

"But I have . . . told Papa," Stephanie went on, "and he said that there was . . . no-one he would rather I . . . married than . . . Kyril."

"He knows your mother has now said you must marry the King?"

"Yes, he knows it . . . but he will do . . . nothing. He

will just let Mama have her way as he . . . always does, and I shall find myself . . . married to that . . . horrible man, when all I . . . want is to be with . . . Kyril."

As if the effort of saying so much had exhausted her, Stephanie laid her head against Laetitia's shoulder and shut her eyes.

The tears were running down her cheeks, and Laetitia wiped them away very gently before she said:

"Try to stop crying, dearest Stephanie, and tell us what has been planned from the very beginning."

"Mama just broke the . . . news to me an . . . hour ago after she had . . . seen the Prime Minister."

Laetitia drew in her breath, knowing that meant it was an official decision of the Cabinet.

"I think he brought her a . . . letter from the King in which he agreed to visit us," Stephanie went on. "Anyway, Mama said: 'I have some good news for you, Stephanie, which I am sure will please you very much. King Viktor of Zvotana is coming here next week and I know he will ask you to be his wife'!"

"What did you do?" Laetitia asked.

"For a moment I found it . . . impossible to . . . speak. I merely gasped, and Mama went on:

"'You are a very fortunate girl, and of course as it will be a State Visit we will give a dinner, a luncheon, and a Ball in his honour, and your engagement will be announced when he is given the Freedom of the City.'"

"And did you say you would not do it?"

"I did not say . . . anything," Stephanie answered, "I just stood looking at Mama, thinking that the . . . ceiling had fallen on my . . . head. Then she walked from the room saying as she went:

"'There is a great deal to be done, and the sooner we get on with it, the better'!"

"Oh, poor Stephanie, how awful for you!" Marie-Henriette exclaimed, and the sympathy in her voice started Stephanie crying once more.

"I cannot . . . bear it!" she said. "Can I get in . . . touch with Kryil and ask . . . him if he will . . . run away with . . . me?"

Laetitia looked at her in surprise. Then she said:

"Would you be prepared to do that?"

Stephanie made a helpless little gesture with her hands.

"I suppose it . . . would be . . . hopeless. Mama would send the Military to fetch me back, and Kyril might be . . . shot or . . . imprisoned for treason! Oh, Laetitia what can I do?"

She was crying again, crying so violently that there was nothing Laetitia could do but hold her very close.

Then as Stephanie went on sobbing, Laetitia looked at Marie-Henriette and said:

"We have to think of something! She will make herself ill!"

Marie-Henriette made the same helpless little gesture which Stephanie had made.

"What can we do?" she asked. "I am sure she is right when she says that if they ran away, Cousin Augustina would have her fetched back and Kyril would be disgraced forever."

"Besides, they would have no money," Laetitia said almost beneath her breath.

"I cannot . . . marry King Viktor . . . I cannot!" Stephanie sobbed. "I have . . . heard about him. He is a . . . horrible man . . . and nobody would want to . . . marry him."

"Why do you say that?" Laetitia asked curiously.

She was trying frantically to remember everything she had heard about King Viktor, which was not very much.

Because they lived so quietly and since their father's death had received very few people of official standing, gossip about the countries adjoining Ovenstadt was not related to her mother.

At the same time, she was aware that nothing would be said when she and her sister were present.

But vaguely at the back of her mind she seemed to remember there was some scandal or other about the King, although for the moment she could not recall what it was.

"I always . . . thought Mama . . . disliked him," Stephanie said, once again wiping the tears from her eyes.

"I remember that when Papa . . . asked if we should invite him to a shooting party last Autumn, Mama said certainly not, he was not only . . . improper but he also had . . . Gypsy blood in his veins."

Laetitia started.

"Did she really say that?"

"Yes, and she crossed him off the list, and instead we had that boring Margrave of Baden-Baden to stay, who Papa said could not hit an . . . elephant at . . . ten yards' range!"

Ordinarily Laetitia would have laughed at this, but Stephanie was so pathetic that it did not even seem amusing.

"So the King has Gypsy blood in his veins, too!" she said.

"It is something Mama has always . . . deprecated and made a . . . terrible fuss about," Stephanie answered. "But a King is a King, and she wants me to be a . . . Queen!"

This brought on another burst of tears, and Laetitia said:

"You have to think, Stephanie. You have to think very carefully what you can do. Of course you cannot marry the King if you love Kyril."

As she spoke she was thinking not only of the Princess but also of her brother.

If Kyril loved Stephanie, which, now that she thought about it, she was sure he did, then she was determined to obtain for him what he wanted, if it was humanly possible with the help or intervention of some magical or Divine power.

After her father, Laetitia loved her brother more than anybody else in the world, and there was a very close resemblance between them.

Kyril was everything Prince Paul would have wanted in a son.

He was handsome, athletic, a magnificent rider, and a sportsman to his fingertips.

What was more, Kyril never had an unkind or ignoble thought, and just as his father had been adored by everybody with whom he came in contact, so was he.

He was loved in the Capital and any other part of the country he visited, and Laetitia had heard how popular he was in his Regiment.

He had certainly already earned a reputation for gallantry, and one of the Generals who had called to see her mother had told her that the men whom Kyril commanded would die rather than let him down.

Princess Olga had been very proud, and Laetitia had cherished the compliment in her heart and thought of it every night when she prayed for her brother's safety and happiness.

Now she thought she had been very obtuse not to have realised long ago that Kyril loved Stephanie.

He had always looked particularly happy when he came back from the Palace after being with her, and it was only because she too had been so happy to be with him that it had never struck her until now that Kyril could love anybody more than his own family.

'It was very foolish of me!' she thought. 'And of course he and Stephanie are perfectly suited.'

Very tall, strong, and masculine, Kyril would want to protect anyone so soft, feminine, and helpless as Stephanie.

Because they had been brought up together, Laetitia had thought of Stephanie almost like another sister, but now she knew that she and Kyril were closely attuned to each other.

There was none of the harsh aggressiveness of her mother in Stephanie, but only the gentleness, kindness, and charm of her father.

But it was one thing to know how happy they would be together and quite another to realise that they had as much chance of being married as she and Marie-Henriette had of getting the wishes they had talked about before Stephanie's arrival.

If the Grand Duchess had set her heart on her daughter becoming a Queen, she would not entertain for one moment the thought of her marrying anyone else.

Whoever was sacrificed, whoever was made miserably unhappy in the process, nothing would alter her decision.

"What can I do . . . Laetitia? P-please . . . please help . . . me," Stephanie was saying.

Laetitia took her arms from her cousin and rose to her feet to stand as she had before looking out the window.

Then she said in a voice that had a note of determination in it:

"We have to do something, and the first step, although I do not know at this moment how, is to prevent the King from proposing to you."

There was silence as she finished speaking.

Then as she turned round she saw that both Stephanie and her sister were staring at her almost in amazement.

Then, as if she had hypnotised them into believing it was possible, Stephanie asked:

"Could you . . . do that? But . . . how? How could you, Laetitia?"

"I do not know yet," Laetitia answered, "but there must be a way, and we have to find it, and quickly!"

Chapter Two

S tephanie suddenly felt frightened and said she
must go home.

"Mama does not know I have come to see . . . you."

"I think it would be a mistake if she found out,"
Laetitia agreed, "but, dearest, try not to be too upset or
unhappy, because I promise you I will do everything I can
to save you."

"Do you mean . . . that?" Stephanie asked.

"If it is humanly possible you shall marry Kyril and not
the King," Laetitia replied.

Stephanie did not answer, but she put her arms round
Laetitia's neck and the tears were back in her eyes. Then
she said:

"I love him! I love him . . . so much that I have to
marry . . . him! But Mama would be very . . . very . . .
angry!"

Because Laetitia knew this was true, there was no use
going on talking about it.

She kissed Stephanie and so did Marie-Henriette,
then tying the ribbons of her bonnet under her chin they
took her to the front door.

Laetitia first looked out to see if there was anybody in
the courtyard, then Stephanie hurried away and started
running as quickly as she could back to the Palace.

Although there were always sentries at the main gates
and outside the front entrance, there were side-doors

which Stephanie and the girls could use where there was no guard.

Laetitia watched her until she was out of sight amongst the shrubs and trees in the garden. Then she shut the front door and went into the Sitting-Room to say to Marie-Henriette:

"I feel as if the world is turning upside-down. Why did we never guess that Kyril and Stephanie loved each other?"

"It does seem strange," Marie-Henriette agreed. "At the same time, Cousin Augustina will never allow them to be married."

"We cannot allow Stephanie to be forced to marry the King when she loves Kyril."

"It would be horrible to be married to anybody one did not love," Marie-Henriette said, "but Papa told me many years ago that that was the penalty for being Royal."

"You talked to Papa about being married?"

"Yes, and he said that while he had been so very lucky to love Mama and be allowed to marry her, it was very unlikely that we should be so fortunate."

"That does not sound like Papa, somehow."

"He was upset at the time because Cousin Carlotta —you remember her?—had been made to marry that horrible Prince of Wurttenberg, and she told Papa how unhappy she was."

When Laetitia thought about it, she realised that nearly all their relatives had been married for political reasons and practically never because they had fallen in love.

When she thought of the Grand Duke and the miserable life he lived with his Prussian wife, she thought the whole thing was humiliating and degrading.

"I really think," she said aloud, "that the anarchists have some point when they wish to abolish the Monarchy."

Marie-Henriette gave a little cry.

"Laetitia, that is a terrible thing to say!"

"Yes, I know," Laetitia agreed, "at the same time I think Stephanie is right. I would rather be dead than married to somebody I did not love."

"She will have the compensation of being a Queen," Marie-Henriette said reflectively.

Laetitia did not answer Marie-Henriette, and she went on:

"At least she will have beautiful gowns to wear, a comfortable Palace in which to live, and lots of delicious food to eat."

Laetitia gave a sigh, but she did not argue.

Marie-Henriette had said things like this before, and she knew that she always deeply resented the change in their circumstances since their father's death and their being so poor that they could never afford a new gown.

As if Laetitia's thoughts communicated themselves to her sister, Marie-Henriette gave a sudden cry.

"Laetitia! I have just thought! If there is a State Ball, Cousin Augustina will have to ask us whether she likes it or not, and we have nothing, absolutely nothing, to wear!"

Laetitia knew this was true, and she said:

"I will speak to Mama, but you know how hard up we are at the moment. There is nothing left to sell except Mama's engagement-ring, and we could not ask her to sell that."

"No, no, of course not," Marie-Henriette agreed.

At the same time, there was a look in her eyes which told Laetitia that she was thinking that diamonds were not much use when there was no-one to see them in the small, confined house in which they now lived.

"I will think of something," Laetitia said quickly, "but first we have to think about Stephanie and her troubles."

"I hope you have not made things worse for her," Marie-Henriette said. "She believes now you will find some magical means of preventing the King from proposing to her. But I expect that when he gets here, Cousin Augustina will have the noose so tight round his neck there will be no escape."

As this was indisputably true, there was nothing Laetitia could say.

She walked into the small Hall, picked up her bonnet, which she had worn for three years, and said:

"I am going to talk to Great-Aunt Aspasia and ask her advice."

"She will not be able to help you," Marie-Henriette answered.

But by the time she had spoken Laetitia had already left the house and was running across the courtyard to a house on the opposite side.

It was larger than theirs, one of the first to be built, and it was where their great-aunt now lived, having been banished from the Palace by the Grand Duke's Prussian wife.

There had been a great deal of bad feeling about it at the time, but Princess Aspasia had settled down as comfortably as she could, with a number of elderly servants to tend her.

Because she found it hard to walk, she was unable to take part in any of the Court ceremonies, but she had in compensation filled her life with gossip.

There was nothing that went on in the Palace, in the Capital, or even in the country itself, that she did not know about.

Her "spy system," for that was what it amounted to, was a mystery to everybody, and yet there was no doubt that she was the best-informed person in the whole of Ovenstadt.

Most people were afraid of her, or else they disliked her as the Grand Duchess did, but Laetitia had always found her fascinating, and she knew now that if anybody could help her it would be the Princess.

She knocked the polished silver knocker on the door, but it was some time before the old Butler had shuffled his feet slowly across the floor to open it.

"Good-morning, Felix!" Laetitia said.

"Why, it's you, Your Highness!" Felix said, peering at her because his sight was failing. "Her Royal Highness'll be delighted to see you."

"Do not bother to announce me," Laetitia said, knowing he had no intention of doing so because it meant going upstairs.

She ran up the staircase and into the Sitting-Room which adjoined the Princess's bedroom.

It was quite a large room compared with other rooms

in the Grace and Favour houses and was packed with an amazing collection of objects that the Princess had collected over her lifetime and from which she would not be parted.

There were innumerable small pieces of china and silver she had received as gifts when she was young, besides a multitude of mementoes.

These included a painting which one of her many relatives had done for her as a child, and several amateur portraits of herself.

There was a case full of the medals which had been worn by her father, and the sword with which one of her brothers had fought in some long-forgotten battle.

There were bunches of dried flowers and bowls of potpourri, and chairs placed very close to where the Princess sat so that she could hear what her visitors were saying despite the fact that she was growing increasingly hard of hearing.

She had been very attractive when she was a young girl, but she had never been beautiful.

Like many Royal Princesses, she had been deliberately kept at home to look after her parents, and since therefore no marriage was arranged for her, she had become an old maid.

However, although she was now nearly eighty, there was nothing old about her mind, and Laetitia found the way in which she spoke so disparagingly about the people she did not like extremely amusing.

"That Woman" was of course the Grand Duchess, and she made no secret of despising the Prime Minister who had climbed into power because the Grand Duchess intrigued with him.

"As you know that King Viktor is coming here," Laetitia said, "I suppose you are also aware that Cousin Augustina intends to marry him to Stephanie."

"I guessed that was her intention," the Princess said. "Has she told the child the fate that is in store for her?"

"Stephanie has just been to see us and she is dreadfully upset," Laetitia replied.

"One of my servants told me she was running through

the garden and was crying," the Princess said. "I suppose you know now that she is in love with your brother."

"You know that too?" Laetitia asked in surprise.

"Of course I know it!" the Princess replied sharply. "You would have seen them mooning about each other all the winter, if you had eyes in your head!"

Laetitia laughed.

"Oh, Great-Aunt Aspasia, there is nobody like you! Now, since you seem to know everything, tell me how I can stop the King from proposing to Stephanie and somehow find a way that she and Kyril can be married."

The expression on the old lady's face changed and now she was not looking mischievous but sad. Instead of speaking, she just shook her head.

"Do you think it is impossible?" Laetitia asked.

"I think it would require a miracle for Kyril and Stephanie ever to get permission to be married. You know 'That Woman' intends her daughter to be a Queen."

"Yes, I know," Laetitia said, "but Stephanie is so desperately unhappy that she says she would rather die than marry the King."

"She will be a Queen, and that will be some compensation," the Princess said sharply.

"That is what Hettie said, but I understand what Stephanie is feeling. I am sure that nothing could make up for the misery of loving one man but having to marry another."

"I agree it complicates things a great deal that Stephanie is in love with Kyril," the Princess replied. "Otherwise she might have been quite happy with the King."

Laetitia looked at her in surprise.

"You say that, but we have always been told that he is horrible."

"That is what 'That Woman' thinks," the Princess replied, "simply because he is somewhat unconventional and not strictly conformable by Prussian standards."

She spoke scathingly and went on:

"Personally, I would like to meet King Viktor. From all I have heard of him, I think we would get on very well."

"What have you heard about him?" Laetitia enquired.

"A great deal that I should not repeat to you," the Princess replied.

Now there was a glint in her eyes which Laetitia knew only too well meant that she knew some amusing and doubtless improper piece of gossip which had been related to her by one of her informers.

"Tell me, please tell me," she begged.

"Why are you so interested?"

"I promised Stephanie I would try to save her."

The Princess made a sound that was half a laugh and half a snort of derision.

"You are taking a great deal upon yourself, my girl," she said. "You had better not let 'That Woman' hear you inciting her daughter to rebellion. You know she expects every decision she makes to be obeyed, and on the double!"

Laetitia laughed as if she could not help it, because as she hated the Grand Duchess it was somehow a consolation to hear her talked about so scathingly by the old Princess.

"If only they could run away!" she said wistfully. "But Stephanie thinks that if they did, the Military would bring them back and Kyril might be imprisoned or even shot for treason."

"That would certainly happen if 'That Woman' had anything to do with it," the Princess said quietly. "You will have to think up something better than that."

"We do not have much time," Laetitia said, following her own thoughts. "The King is arriving in a week. That brings us to Thursday."

"That is correct," the Princess replied. "I hear he is going to drive or ride from his Palace in Zvotana, which will take him all day, and stay the night at Thor Castle in the mountains."

Laetitia gave a little exclamation.

"I never thought of that! Of course! It is obvious that is where he will stay."

She knew and loved Thor Castle because every year during her childhood her father and the Grand Duke used to take their families to the Castle for holidays, especially in the winter.

As the Grand Duchess disliked the cold and was always busy seeing to State Affairs in the Capital, she used to stay behind.

For Laetitia and for the others it had always been a gloriously happy time, with nobody to find fault with them and dozens of exciting things to do.

The Grand Duke and her father would climb the snow-capped mountains which towered above them or drop down a few hundred feet to ride where it was possible on more level ground.

For the children there was tobogganing on the snow-covered slopes, and what Kyril enjoyed more than anything else was to climb the walls of the Castle itself.

Laetitia was always nervous when he took dangerous risks as he clambered up the towers on the outside or walked precariously on the cresselated battlements to show he was not afraid of heights.

In the evenings because the Grand Duchess was not there they would sing and dance in the great Baronial Hall with its huge fireplace burning whole trees.

Princess Olga would play the piano for the three girls and the two boys, Kyril and Prince Otto, to dance the wild Gypsy dances which they had watched and learnt ever since they were small.

Sometimes they would act Charades or even a Play which Laetitia would write and produce, and which would always be highly dramatic and amusing, although sometimes unintentionally.

It was only when her father died that their holidays in the Castle ceased.

Laetitia knew that the Grand Duchess had deliberately stopped their going there as she had put an end to every other amusement she could where Prince Paul's family was concerned.

"Of course," Laetitia said aloud, "that is where the King will stay, and I only hope he . . . appreciates it. Papa loved the Castle."

The note in her voice told the Princess how much she missed the old days, and she said:

"I doubt if he will appreciate anything when he comes

down from the clouds to meet 'That Woman' and learn what is expected of him in Ovenstadt."

"As the King is very important and reigns over a much bigger country than ours," Laetitia said, "I cannot think why he has to come here to upset everything and obey Cousin Augustina, if that is what he is going to do."

"As I can imagine you are very curious about him," the Princess said, "I will tell you what I know, or rather, what it is advisable for you to hear."

"Please tell me everything," Laetitia pleaded. "I am thinking frantically of how I can save Stephanie, and I cannot do it unless you help me."

"King Viktor," the Princess began, "is, from all I have heard, having a lot of trouble in Zvotana at the moment."

"Why is that?" Laetitia asked.

"He inherited the throne only three years ago," the Princess answered. "Previous to that, owing to an extremely incompetent and stupid Regent, the country had got very out-of-hand."

"In what way?"

"There were revolutionaries working up the people against the Monarchy, both politically and financially they were in a mess, and King Viktor, who had been educated in France, was pitch-forked into a situation which might have appalled any young man."

"Then he is quite young!" Laetitia exclaimed. "I thought he would be at least thirty!"

"I will say one thing about you, Laetitia, you have a quick brain. He will be thirty next birthday, but he had not expected to inherit because he was not the son of the last King, but his nephew."

"And what happened to the Crown Prince?"

"Boris was quite young when his father died, which was why there was a Regent. Then, just when he was ready to take over power on his twenty-first birthday, he was involved in a duel."

Laetitia was listening wide-eyed as the Princess went on:

"Of course it should never have been allowed to

happen, except that the Regent was a nincompoop and had no idea what was happening until it was too late."

"And the Crown Prince was killed?"

"Stone dead, and all over some actress with whom he should not have become involved in the first place."

"It must have caused a great scandal," Laetitia said.

"I am certain the Courts of Europe talked of nothing else," the Princess agreed drily, "but of course it was hushed up as much as possible, and Viktor, who was in Paris enjoying himself, was dragged back at a moment's notice, crowned, and told to rule over a Kingdom he had not seen for several years."

The Princess gave a little laugh as she said:

"I have always felt sorry for the poor man, and I imagine the last three years have been exceedingly unpleasant for him."

"Then why has Cousin Augustina been saying until now that he was horrible and she would not have him to stay at the Palace, and also that he had Gypsy blood in him?"

"You are too young to be given the answer to the first part of your question," the Princess said, but her eyes were twinkling.

"You mean Cousin Augustina thought the King was immoral?"

"He had been enjoying himself in France, and he saw no reason to alter his ways simply because he had become King! Needless to say, there were plenty of lovely ladies of every class only too willing to amuse him and take his mind off matters of State."

"That would certainly shock Cousin Augustina!" Laetitia remarked.

"If there is one place that is dull and boring to the point where even death is preferable," the Princess said, "it is the type of Prussian Court which 'That Woman' has tried to instal here."

She gave a sigh as she said:

"The Palace was always a place of laughter when my father was the Grand Duke, and the Ovenstadts are a happy people if they are left alone."

"That is what Papa used to say."

"Your father was a true Ovenstadt," the Princess replied. "They sing, they dance, and because they are happy they want everybody else to be happy too."

She made an expressive gesture with her blue-veined hand as she finished:

"If you tried to explain what I have just told you to That Woman,' she would have no idea what you were talking about."

"Go on about the King," Laetitia pleaded.

"In answer to the second part of your question," the Princess said, "of course he has Gypsy blood in him, just as there is the same blood in this family."

"Cousin Augustina says that is untrue."

"She believes what she wants to believe," the Princess replied, "but you, my child, are beautiful because you have the black hair of our Gypsy ancestor."

"I am so glad that you believe in the legend," Laetitia said. "I have never liked to ask you about it before because I should have been so disappointed if you had said it was untrue!"

"Of course it is true!" the Princess said sharply. "My great-great-grandfather took his wife to every Doctor, quack, and Spa before he came home and allowed a Gypsy to produce what he was incapable of doing."

The Princess spoke without thinking; then, remembering how young and innocent Laetitia was, she said quickly:

"It was magic, of course, it was magic, and the son who was born to my great-great-grandmother was, I understand, so handsome that the Ladies of the Court could never take their eyes from him, and many of them fainted if he spoke to them!"

Laetitia clapped her hands together.

"I am so glad you have told me that. It is what I have always believed, and it makes us all seem very romantic."

Then, as if she remembered Stephanie's problems, she said:

"Now please tell me how the King has Gypsy blood in him."

"His connection is nearer than ours," the Princess replied, "because his great-grandfather actually married a Gypsy."

"Married her!" Laetitia exclaimed.

"She was a Russian Gypsy, and the Russians have always treated their Gypsies far better than other Europeans have. Because they can dance and sing so superbly, the Grand Dukes and Princes of Russia have always outbid one another in engaging them to appear in their houses and private Theatres."

She paused, realised that Laetitia was listening wide-eyed, and went on:

"King Viktor's great-grandmother, Saviya, was the most famous Gypsy dancer there has ever been. She danced before the Tsar, and the King of Zvotana who was staying with him in St. Petersburg fell madly in love with her."

"And she agreed to marry him?"

"Gypsies, as I expect you know, are in their own way very strict in their morals. Saviya refused to become the King's mistress, since she intended, I suspect, to marry eventually a man of her own tribe."

"But instead she married the King!"

"Legend has it that they were blissfully happy, but when he brought her home to Zvotana there was, as you can imagine, much consternation and criticism, and a number of his relatives refused to accept her."

"What happened?"

"She died giving birth to their first child, who was a daughter."

"How sad!" Laetitia said.

"The King, I believe, was broken-hearted, but of course he had to marry again and produced an heir, who eventually succeeded him and whose grandson Boris was, as I have already told you, killed in a duel."

"What happened to Saviya's daughter?" Laetitia asked

"By a twist of fate, or perhaps Gypsy magic," the Princess replied, "she married a cousin of the King, and they had a daughter who married Boris's uncle, the younger brother of the late King. Their son was Viktor, who thus succeeded his uncle when Boris was killed."

"It is a fascinating story," Laetitia said. "And does he look like a Gypsy?"

The Princess smiled.

"That is one question I cannot answer, for I have never seen him, but if your family is anything to go by, the Gypsy strain should have made him as handsome as Kyril."

The Princess's words brought Laetitia's mind back to the problem of Kyril and Stephanie.

"However handsome the King may be," she said almost as if she spoke to herself, "it would be impossible for Stephanie to love him as much as she loves my brother."

"That may be indisputably true," the Princess said, "but Royalty have to marry whom they are told to marry, and 'That Woman' will see to it that Stephanie is unable to defy her."

"There must be something we can do to stop it," Laetitia said desperately.

"I wish I could help you, my child."

The Princess paused for a moment. Then she went on:

"What I will do is to find out all I can about King Viktor's feelings in the matter."

"Why should he want to marry Stephanie, whom he has never seen?" Laetitia asked.

"He has seen a portrait of her."

"How do you know that?"

Before the Princess could reply, Laetitia gave a little cry.

"Of course! I remember Stephanie was being painted a month or so ago."

"Exactly!" the Princess said. "It was 'That Woman's' idea to send it to Zvotana, although I understand that at the time, she told Stephanie that she was having it painted as a present for the Grand Duke."

"Stephanie looked very pretty in her portrait," Laetitia pondered, "but that still does not explain why the King should wish to be married to her."

"I think it is a case of a Roman Circus," the Princess said drily.

Because Laetitia was well read, she was aware that when Roman Rulers wanted to divert the people's minds from some reversal they had suffered on the battlefield, or from the privations which they were suffering, they put on magnificent exhibitions in the Circus Maximus, consisting of dramatic performances, chariot races, and hunting of wild beasts.

They kept those who watched them from thinking of their own troubles and instead kept their minds on the shows, which excited them, and later the phrase was used by other nations to describe political diversions.

"So Stephanie's and the King's marriage is to be a Roman Circus for Zvotana," Laetitia said.

"The women of every country enjoy a wedding," the Princess replied, "and you will see that here the crowds will forget, for one day at least, how much they dislike 'That Woman' and the new laws and taxes which are being imposed on them in poor Louis's name."

Laetitia looked at her great-aunt in surprise.

"Do the people really dislike Cousin Augustina as much as we do?"

"A good deal more," the Princess replied, "and if Zvotana needs a Roman Circus, so do we in Ovenstadt."

"I had no idea it was as bad as that!" Laetitia said.

"The Prime Minister's policy has put up the cost of living in an almost astronomical way, and when the people are hungry they rebel."

"Rebel?" Laetitia gasped.

"I only wish Louis would realize what is going on!" the Princess went on.

"Could Mama perhaps talk to him?"

"I have thought of that," the Princess answered, "for I believe she is the only person who could make him realise that he must assert himself and stop the rot before it is too late."

"Then why do you not tell her what you are saying to me?" Laetitia enquired.

The Princess paused for a moment before she said:

"I have thought of it, my dear, I have thought of it for a long time. But I know how much you are suffering already because of 'That Woman's' dislike of you and her jealousy, and it might only complicate things even more."

Laetitia knew without the Princess saying it that if their Cousin Augustina suspected that the Grand Duke was talking politics with her mother, she would somehow make things very uncomfortable for both of them.

"Then what can we do?" she asked.

"Enjoy the Roman Circus, I suppose!" the Princess replied.

"No, no!" Laetitia cried. "We cannot be so limp as to do nothing and make both Stephanie and Kyril unhappy for the rest of their lives."

The Princess smiled.

"You sound just like your father when he wanted to help somebody, which was something he never failed to do."

"If Papa were here now," Laetitia said, "he would say we must not sit back and let two people suffer through no fault of their own."

"I am sure he would," the Princess agreed, "but even he might find it difficult to find a solution this time."

"There must be one!" Laetitia said firmly. "And as today is Tuesday we have exactly a week from tomorrow before the King arrives at Thor Castle."

She spoke with an intense little note in her voice, and watching her the Princess thought how beautiful she was.

"Too beautiful to be shut away in that pokey little house across the courtyard," she told herself, "and far too beautiful for 'That Woman' to tolerate!"

Suddenly she felt very old and useless.

Then with a perception which sometimes comes to old people when they are nearing the end of their lives, she said almost without thinking:

"I do not know how you can do it, but I have an idea, my child, that because you are so determined and because you are fighting for what is right, you will find a way to help Stephanie and Kyril!"

* * *

Going back to her own house, Laetitia felt as if the

Princess's words were ringing in her ears, like a trumpet-call summoning her to action.

And yet her brain seemed full of cotton-wool, so that she could not think even how to begin the task she had set herself.

After they had finished luncheon, a meagre meal which they consumed without noticing what they ate because they were preoccupied in talking about Stephanie's marriage, Laetitia said:

"I think, Mama, I will go riding this afternoon."

"Of course, dearest," Princess Olga agreed, "but Gustave must accompany you. You know how it shocks Cousin Augustina if you ride alone."

"Gustave is growing so old that he finds it hard just to look after the horses, so why should I take him on a tiring ride as well?" Laetitia replied. "I will keep well out of sight of the Palace, Mama, and hope Cousin Augustina does not see me, nor any of her spying servants who report to her whatever I do."

The Princess sighed, but she did not say anything.

They all knew that the Grand Duchess had introduced into the Palace a number of Prussian servants who reported to her everything that was going on, especially, Laetitia was sure, anything that concerned Prince Paul's family.

However, she went to the stables at the back of the house, where they had only two horses left from the number her father had kept when he was alive.

They had to sell all their horses when they moved into the Grace and Favour House except for two very young stallions which were extremely well bred and for which the Prince had had great hopes when he acquired them.

Now he would have been pleased to see that his judgement had been right, for both horses were superlative in their own way and were an endless delight to Laetitia and Marie-Henriette when Kyril was not at home.

Then, unless he could borrow a mount from the Palace, he monopolised the horses, and they had little chance of riding them until he returned to his Regiment.

Now Laetitia, in a very becoming but almost threadbare riding-habit which she had worn for years, mounted the stallion which was called *Kaho*.

It was a name which the Grand Duchess would certainly have disapproved of if she had been aware of it, because it meant "Chief" in Romany.

It had amused Prince Paul to give all his horses Gypsy names, and *Kaho*, Laetitia thought, looked like a Chief, and certainly he performed like one.

She rode out of the stables at the back of the Grace and Favour Houses and, moving at once away as far as possible from the Palace, kept in the shade of the trees until she was well away from the City and out into the open country.

Then, as she galloped down into the valley, she thought as she always did how beautiful Ovenstadt was and how much she loved it.

In the distance there was the range of mountains which they shared with Zvotana. They extended a considerable distance, making a natural boundary between them and other, less friendly countries.

Some of the mountains were so high that there was always even in the hottest summer a touch of snow in the crevices and on the peaks. Now, since spring was only just ending, their peaks were gleaming white against the blue of the sky.

The snows were responsible for the profusion of wild flowers in the grassland through which the river flowed.

Their colour was to Laetitia so beautiful that she felt it was wrong for *Kaho*'s hoofs to trample on them.

A cloud of butterflies diverted her attention and they seemed to her like fairy-creatures fluttering in front of her as she rode *Kaho* through the thick grass.

As they drew away from the City, she began looking to right and left in search of what she was seeking.

Because of what the Princess had said about the Gypsy blood of the King, she was sure that the only chance of finding a solution to her problems and difficulties was through the Gypsies.

Perhaps they would have some magic spell she could

use on the King, or perhaps they would give her the inspiration she did not have at the moment.

Whatever it was, some instinct so strong that she could not help obeying it drove her in search of them.

Surprisingly, because at this time of the year there were usually plenty of Gypsies to be seen, she had ridden for nearly an hour before she glimpsed in the distance what she sought.

There was no mistaking the round tops of the painted caravans and the Gypsies moving round them.

She hoped she had found an important tribe and, if possible, an Hungarian one.

Hungary bordered Ovenstadt on the East, and the Hungarian Gypsies, although they had often been persecuted and abused, were more intelligent and certainly of an older lineage than many others Laetitia had met.

In Hungary the Chief of the tribe was called "a Duke of Little Egypt," and the King of Hungary had at one time given the Gypsies letters of protection.

As she drew nearer, Laetitia thought deep in her heart that she was certainly in luck, because she knew before she reached them that the Gypsies she had seen in the distance were not only Hungarians but specifically Kalderash.

They were exactly what she was hoping she would find, for the Kalderash were not only the metal-workers who fashioned the magnificent gold goblets that the nobles in Hungary used to ornament their tables, besides working in every other metal, but they were also the Gypsies most concerned with magic.

"That is what I want," she told herself.

As she rode forward, sure of a welcome because they would know who she was, she felt her heart beating excitedly, almost as if already her instinct was telling her how she could save Stephanie.

There were eight caravans, some of them very elaborate and painted in brilliant colours.

As Laetitia appeared, a number of dark-skinned faces turned towards her and suspicious black eyes regarded her for a moment questioningly.

They were, Laetitia saw, a collection of exceedingly

good-looking Gypsies. In fact, with their high cheek-bones, black eyes, and dark hair, the women were beautiful and the men handsome.

They were Hungarian, but she thought they also had Russian blood in them.

As Laetitia approached them slowly, one of the women must have recognised her, for she heard her say some words in Romany which included her name.

Instantly the faces turned towards her were smiling, and the children with their large gazelle-like eyes were running towards her.

Laetitia brought her horse to a standstill.

"Good-day!" she said to them in Romany. "I wish to speak to your *Voivode*."

Because she spoke their language, several of the women, with red handkerchiefs over their heads and huge gold ear-rings dangling from their ears, clapped their hands and exclaimed in delight.

Then one of the Gypsy boys ran to a caravan surrounded by the others, and a moment later a tall man appeared who Laetitia knew by his bearing and his clothes was a Duke of Little Egypt.

He wore a blue coat and very high boots. On his short jacket he had a number of gold buttons, and there was a heavy gold chain hung with a pendant round his neck.

He carried in his hand a staff called *bare esti robli rupui*, which Laetitia knew was the last remaining link with a King's sceptre.

It was made entirely of silver, and the hilt, octagonal in shape, was adorned with a red tassle.

The staff was engraved, although she could not see it at the moment, with the *Semno*, or authentic sign of the Gypsies, comprising the five ritual figures.

As he came towards her Laetitia dismounted, and instantly two boys of about sixteen went to *Kaho's* head.

Then she walked through the watching crowd of Gypsies to the *Voivode* and held out her hand.

"I think you know that I am Princess Laetitia of Ovenstadt," she said, "and I would like, if it is possible, to speak to you alone."

He bowed as he took her hand, and she realised it was a greeting that was not subservient but that of an equal.

"I should be honoured, Your Highness," he said, speaking her language.

They walked through the caravans to where, outside a more highly decorated one, stood a chair.

The *Voivode* snapped his fingers, and a Gypsy boy hurried to bring another chair and set it down beside the one that was already there.

"Will Your Highness be seated?" the *Voivode* enquired.

Laetitia did so and he sat beside her.

"Where are you going?" she asked.

"Not to your City, if that is what Your Highness suspects."

"I was not thinking that," Laetitia answered, "and I can only apologise for the new laws that prevent you from moving freely in my country as you have always been able to do in the past. I know it would have distressed my father, Prince Paul."

"His Highness is greatly missed," the *Voivode* replied, "but we are surprised that the Grand Duke should allow a Prussian woman to revoke the hospitality we have always enjoyed here."

"She does not believe, as we do, that we are of your blood," Laetitia said.

She spoke deliberately and saw by the expression in the *Voivode*'s eyes that he was not only pleased with what she said but also surprised that she should admit it.

"We of the Rákónzi family have a Gypsy ancestor," Laetitia said, "and King Viktor of Zvotana is also of Gypsy descent."

The *Voivode* nodded his head as if he was aware of that already.

"And now I want to ask you a great favour."

"Your Highness has but to ask."

Quietly and in a few words Laetitia told him what she wanted, and when he agreed, she said:

"Thank you, I am very grateful!"

"Because, as you say, we are joined by blood," the

Voivode said, "I hope you will accept our hospitality, and as it is too early in the day for a meal, may I offer Your Highness a glass of wine?"

"Thank you," Laetitia answered.

She thought it would offend him if she refused, and she was aware that it was a great honour to be invited to drink with the *Voivode*.

Most Gypsy tribes kept very much to themselves, and only in exceptional circumstances were outsiders permitted to join them at a meal.

The *Voivode* rose, went to the door of the caravan, and spoke rapidly in Romany to somebody inside.

A moment later, two exquisite goblets filled with wine and fashioned in gold and ornamented with semi-precious stones were handed out to him by somebody who remained inside.

Laetitia could see only that she wore large rings on her fingers and her wrists were weighted down with heavy gold bracelets from which hung a number of golden coins.

The *Voivode* took the goblets and presented one of them to Laetitia. It was so beautiful that she could not help exclaiming:

"I have never seen anything so exquisite! Did your people make this?"

"We have copied them," the *Voivode* replied, "but these actual cups have belonged in my family for generations and are famous among the Kalderash for their unusual workmanship."

"I am sure most people would think it strange that you should possess anything not only so beautiful but so valuable."

"If you are thinking of ordinary thieves," the *Voivode* replied, "they would be too frightened of being cursed to touch anything of ours. It is only the Military who treat us brutally, but sometimes even they are afraid."

"They are afraid of your magic," Laetitia said slowly, "and that is what I need to help me now."

"I will consider what you have told me," the *Voivode* replied.

"Then please help, if it is possible," Laetitia pleaded.

"I think you know already that your blood has called to mine, and what we are capable of giving you is at your disposal," the *Voivode* said.

It was as if he rebuked her for doubting him, and Laetitia answered humbly:

"Forgive me, but there is so much happiness at stake, and I cannot help feeling it is wrong for people to be made unhappy for no reason except greed and a desire for power."

She was thinking of the Grand Duchess as she spoke, and as if the *Voivode* read her thoughts he said quietly:

"She is evil, but for those who believe, we have a magic that is stronger than the powers of darkness."

"I believe that, I promise you I believe that," Laetitia said.

The *Voivode* smiled as if what she said pleased him.

"I know that what you have told me, Your Highness, comes from your heart," he said, "and the magic we, the Kalderash, can perform is based on the power that comes from love."

As if there was no more to say, he drained his goblet, and because instinctively Laetitia knew what was expected of her, she did the same.

The wine was sweet and smooth and somehow different from any wine she had drunk before.

It seemed to move almost like sunshine into her body, and she wondered if that too was magic—what the peasants would think of as a "love-potion."

Then she smiled at the absurdity of the idea, and as she rose she said:

"Thank you once again for your kindness, your hospitality, and your promise."

He took her hand in his. Then he said:

"Go in peace. The way will be shown to you, then your heart must follow it."

He spoke very solemnly, almost as if he was blessing her, and without thinking it was a strange thing to do, Laetitia curtseyed to him.

Then as she moved to where *Kaho* was waiting for her, it might have been the wine, but she felt as if the sunshine was unexpectedly golden, and she felt ecstatically happy.

Chapter Three

As Laetitia came into the courtyard she saw outside their house a carriage bearing the insignia of the Grand Duke.

She went through the front door and walked not into the small Drawing-Room at the front but into the Dining-Room at the back.

It was a very small room, separated from the Drawing-Room by a thick curtain which could be pulled aside to make more space if there was a party.

In fact, of course, as they could never afford to give a party, the curtain was seldom drawn, but Laetitia knew she would be able to hear if it was the Grand Duke who was with her mother.

For one terrifying moment she had thought it might be the Grand Duchess.

Because she had been so busy these past few days, intriguing to help Stephanie, she was always afraid that the Grand Duchess would learn what was happening and make a terrible scene.

Then to her relief she heard the deep voice of the Grand Duke as he said:

"It is intolerable, but there is nothing I can do about it!"

Laetitia stiffened, wondering what had happened now to make him speak like that.

"I am so sorry for you, Louis dear," Princess Olga

replied, "and I cannot believe that Augustina really plans to do anything so unconventional."

"She is determined to assert her authority," the Grand Duke said bitterly, "and that is not all."

"What else?" Princess Olga enquired.

"On the last day of the King's visit," the Grand Duke replied, "he will receive the Freedom of the City. As you know, Olga, it has always been traditional for this to be handed to the recipient by whoever is on the throne."

"Yes, of course," Princess Olga replied. "I remember when the Emperor of Austria came here what an impressive ceremony it was and how well you performed it."

"That is what I supposed was intended this time."

"It has been changed?"

"My wife insists that she will drive to the Civic Hall with Otto," the Grand Duke replied, "that he and she will receive the King when he arrives, and that she herself will present His Majesty with the Key to the City."

There was a pause in which Laetitia knew her mother was staring at the Grand Duke in sheer astonishment.

"But where will you be?" she asked at length.

"I am expected to take my wife's place in the carriage with King Viktor," the Grand Duke replied, "and as by then he will have proposed to Stephanie, she will drive with us."

Laetitia held her breath. Then her mother said:

"It is intolerable, Louis! I cannot bear you to be humiliated in such a way. You must refuse to allow Augustina to push you aside so blatantly."

"I have already argued with her until I am tired of the sound of my own voice," the Grand Duke replied. "But she is determined, and nothing I say or do will alter her mind."

There was a silence, then Princess Olga said with almost a sob in her voice:

"I am sorry, so very, very sorry, dear Louis. I wish I could help you."

"You do help me," the Grand Duke replied, "because you are the only person who understands; the only person I can talk to."

Because now he was speaking in a very different tone,

Laetitia felt it was wrong for her to go on eavesdropping when they were talking intimately.

She went from the Dining-Room and up the stairs to her bedroom.

As she did so, she thought that the King's proposed visit had upset everybody.

First Stephanie was in despair, and she knew that when Kyril arrived tomorrow with his Regiment, which would be on duty, he would be as desperate as she was when he learnt they must be parted.

Now the Grand Duke also was humiliated and upset, and that meant her mother would be too.

"How can one woman cause so much trouble?" Laetitia asked herself, and knew that she hated the Grand Duchess as much as the Gypsies did.

She locked her door and drew from the bottom drawer of a chest a gown on which she had been working every minute that she had to herself.

It was a Gypsy dress she had worn three years ago the last time they had been at Thor Castle.

She had then written a Gypsy Play to amuse her father and the Grand Duke, in which they all had acted.

Afterwards they had danced round an imitation fire in the centre of the ancient Baronial Hall to the Gypsy tunes her mother played on the piano.

The Grand Duke and her father had applauded the whole performance but especially, Laetitia remembered, her dancing.

She had practised very hard before they went to the Castle and had even, without her mother and father being aware of it, crept out in the evenings to watch the Gypsies who had camped near them.

She had memorised their steps and gestures and the brilliant manner in which they leapt round and over their fire.

The dress she had worn for the performance in Thor Castle she had bought in the City, and had then asked one of the maids to add to it the glittering gold beads, sequins, and ribbons with which the Gypsies embellished their skirts and blouses.

Only the tight-fitting velvet bodice was not decorated, and Laetitia knew that because she had such a slim figure, the dress when she wore it made her look very sylph-like and at the same time alluring.

There was a red veil to wear over her hair. It had gold coins hanging from it, which jingled when she danced, as did the bracelets on both her wrists and ankles, which were tied with red ribbons.

She knew that often the jewellery worn by the Gypsies was real, but at least her stage effect was a good imitation.

It was unlikely that anybody would expect her to own real gold coins and precious stones as many of the Kalderash women did.

Because she had been much younger when she last wore the dress, she not only had to let it out but also to lengthen it. Being skilful with her needle, Laetitia thought when she had finished that the dress looked even better than it had before.

She worked on it for an hour, then put it away in a drawer, locking it just in case someone should find it inadvertently.

Then she went downstairs, knowing by looking out the window that the Grand Duke's carriage had left and he was therefore no longer with her mother.

She found her sitting in the Drawing-Room, looking sad.

"I heard you come back, dearest," she said, "but as you know, Cousin Louis was here with me."

"I expect he came to tell you his troubles, Mama."

"I wish I could help him," Princess Olga said. "I cannot bear to see a man who is so kind and intelligent as Louis being so unhappy."

"I think all arranged marriages are wicked!" Laetitia said, thinking of Stephanie. "Nothing, Mama, would ever make me marry a man I did not love."

The Princess was still for a moment. Then she said:

"I keep wondering, my dearest, if you will ever have a chance to marry anybody, living as we do here."

Because her mother sounded so worried, Laetitia kissed her and said:

"Do not be depressed, Mama. Perhaps if Cousin Augustina is obliged to ask us to the State Ball, there will be some handsome Prince Charming who will fall in love either with me or with Hettie."

Her mother did not answer, and Laetitia knew what she was thinking. Now that her father was dead, they were so unimportant that it was extremely unlikely that any member of another Royal Family would ask for their hands in marriage.

It was a depressing thought, and as she walked from her mother's side she caught a glimpse of herself in a mirror hanging on the wall and knew without being in the least conceited that she looked very lovely.

"And also like a Gypsy," she added to herself, "and that will certainly lower my chances."

Then, because the sun was shining through the windows, she thought it was not important and there was no use being depressed.

Her father had often said: "Something will turn up," and perhaps, like the miracle she was trying to find for Stephanie, there would be a miracle for her and Hettie as well.

Because she did not want to think of herself when her mother was feeling depressed, she said:

"I am sure, Mama, that Cousin Louis went away feeling better because you were kind and understanding towards him. If only 'That Woman,' as Great-Aunt Aspasia calls her, were not at the Palace, we would be able to go there as we used to do."

"Have you seen the Princess?" her mother asked. "That reminds me—I ought to call on her. I feel she must be very lonely."

"She is far too clever for that," Laetitia replied. "Great-Aunt Aspasia knows everything that is going on in the Palace, in the City, in the country, and everywhere else in Europe! And that keeps her interested."

Princess Olga laughed.

"That is quite true. She has always been the same—an inveterate gossip, but such fun to be with. I must tell Louis to visit her. It might cheer him up."

"Yes, do that, Mama," Laetitia agreed. "And of course she knew that Stephanie was to marry the King before even Stephanie herself knew about it!"

She paused; then, because she thought her mother ought to know, Laetitia said very quietly:

"She also knew, as we did not, that Stephanie is in love with Kyril!"

There was a silence in which Laetitia found it hard to look at her mother. Then the Princess said in a strangled tone:

"I hoped nobody knew that . . . except me!"

"You knew, Mama?"

"Yes, of course," Princess Olga replied, "and when I realised that Kyril was falling in love with her, I prayed that while he was away, as he has been these last months, he would forget her."

"Stephanie is quite certain he loves her as much as she loves him."

"That is true," Princess Olga said in a frightened voice, "but it must at all costs be kept from Cousin Augustina. If she thought Kyril was interfering with her plans for Stephanie, I am sure she would do everything she could to ruin his life."

She gave a sudden cry of horror.

"I know what she would do!"

"What, Mama?"

"She talked of it last year, but I do not think it was because of Stephanie."

"What was she suggesting?" Laetitia asked, and her voice was tense.

Princess Olga drew in her breath.

"Cousin Augustina thought it would be a good idea if Kyril and Otto went to Prussia for a year to train at the Prussian Army Barracks."

Laetitia gave an exclamation of horror, and the Princess went on:

"The only think that prevented it from happening was that the Grand Duke told her how severely the cadets are treated, the duels they are forced to fight, and the brutal way they are punished if they do anything wrong."

The Princess's voice trembled as she added almost in a whisper:

"How could I bear the thought of Kyril having to endure such treatment? And yet I feel sure that if Cousin Augustina is annoyed with him, that is where he will be sent, whether Otto goes with him or not."

"It is something that must never happen, Mama," Laetitia said.

"He must be careful, very careful," Princess Olga went on. "When he returns tomorrow, you must talk to him, Laetitia, and warn him, as I shall do."

"Yes, of course, Mama," Laetitia agreed, "and try not to worry."

At the same time, she felt that the Grand Duchess was like a dark cloud blotting out the sunshine from their life and menacing them all with a fear that seemed to seep insidiously into her mind.

* * *

Kyril arrived home the following afternoon, looking exceedingly handsome in his smart uniform, and so much like his father that Laetitia felt not only inexpressible joy that he had returned, but also a pang of sorrow that their father was not with them.

Then as Kyril hugged first his mother, then Laetitia, and lastly Marie-Henriette, and his laughter seemed to fill the small house, it was impossible to think of anything but the joy of having him with them.

"I thought it would be another three months before I could see you all again," he said. "It was a great piece of luck that King Viktor should wish to pay us a State Visit."

The way he spoke told Laetitia that he had no idea of the underlying reason for the King's visit.

She waited until they had heard about the manoeuvres Kyril's Regiment had been doing in the mountains, the new apparatus they had for swinging the guns across deep gullies, the peaks they had climbed, and the horses he had been riding.

Then, when Princess Olga said she must go to change for dinner and Marie-Henriette went with her, Laetitia was alone with her brother.

"I want a bath," he said. "I suppose it is possible to have one?"

"Yes, of course," Laetitia replied. "In fact, Gertrude, who expected you would want one, has been heating the water all day."

Kyril laughed.

"Dear old Gertrude, I knew she would be thinking of me," he said. "I will go to the kitchen and give her a kiss."

Gertrude was the old maid who had been with them since they were children and had always spoilt Kyril because he was her favourite.

"Before you go, Kyril," Laetitia said quickly, "I have something to tell you."

"What is it?" Kyril asked. "And by the way, you are looking exceedingly pretty! The Officers in my Regiment will all be congratulating me if they catch sight of you during the festivities."

Laetitia drew in her breath.

"Do you know what the festivities are really for?"

"For King Viktor, I suppose," her brother replied.

With what was a considerable effort, Laetitia managed to say:

"Cousin Augustina has asked him here to . . . arrange for him to marry Stephanie!"

She could hardly bear to look at the shock in her brother's eyes and then the expression of pain which swept away his smile and made him in the passing of a second immeasurably older.

"Is that true?" he asked hoarsely.

"That is what Cousin Augustina has planned, and Stephanie, as you can imagine, is desperately unhappy."

"She told you that we love each other?"

"Yes, she came here in tears. But, Kyril, what is more important than anything else is that Cousin Augustina must not have the slightest idea that you love each other."

"Damn her!" Kyril said violently. "She does not care about Stephanie's feelings, she just wants her to be as powerful as she herself has always wanted to be!"

"Yes, I know," Laetitia replied, "but if she has the

slightest idea that Stephanie loves you, Mama says you will be sent to Prussia."

She saw the expression of horror on her brother's face. Then he said in a voice she had never heard him use before:

"If I cannot marry Stephanie, it does not matter where I go or what I do."

Because she could not bear him to sound so despondent, Laetitia rose and took his hand in hers.

"Listen, Kyril," she said, "I am going to try by every means in my power to prevent the King, when he comes here, from proposing to Stephanie. I am not quite certain at the moment how I can do it, but I am praying I shall be successful."

She paused before she added slowly:

"Then at least it will give both you and her time to think of what can be . . . done in the . . . future."

"There is no future for us, I know that in my heart," Kyril said.

"Cousin Louis told Stephanie that he would rather have you for his son-in-law than anybody else he knew."

Her brother looked at her in surprise. Then he asked:

"Did he really say that?"

"Stephanie says so, and if we can prevent anyone more important from asking to marry her, perhaps in time you will have a chance."

"Not if Cousin Augustina has anything to do with it," Kyril said bitterly. "She hates us all—Otto told me so—and I think she would rather Stephanie married a grizzly bear than me!"

"Surely you are prepared to . . . fight to make her your . . . wife?"

"I would fight for her and die for her," Kyril answered. "I love her, Laetitia, as I could never love anybody else."

"I know that."

He paused before he added:

"Papa loved Mama in the same way. He said that from the first moment he saw her it was impossible ever again to see another woman's face."

"They were so blissfully happy," Laetitia said, "even

though we were very poor, but not as . . . poor as we are now."

Kyril did not answer, and after a moment she said, as if she must impress on him the danger:

"Things will be worse, very much worse, if the Grand Duchess has the slightest suspicion of what you and Stephanie feel for each other. Oh, Kyril, for our . . . sakes as well as your own . . . please be . . . careful!"

"You know I will," Kyril said. "But now that I am back, you will have to help me, Laetitia."

"What do you want me to do?"

"First of all, I want to see Stephanie, and alone."

"That is going to be difficult."

"Can you take her a message to ask her to meet me in the place we have met before, and where we have never been discovered so far?"

"Oh, Kyril, where is it?"

There was a sudden twinkle in her brother's eyes as he said:

"I bet you could never guess."

"Tell me."

"On the roof of the Palace!"

"Kyril, what an extraordinary place to meet!"

"That is what anybody else would think," he replied, "and that is why it is safe."

"But how do you get there?"

"I have climbed over that roof ever since I was a small boy," he said, "just as we used to climb up Thor Castle. In fact, the Palace is much easier."

"And of course," Laetitia said, as if she was speaking to herself, "it is easier for Stephanie to leave her room and go upwards than it is to go down, where she would be seen by the footmen on duty."

"Exactly!" Kyril said. "So, give her the message as soon as you can, and do not forget."

"Of course I will," Laetitia said, "but promise me by everything you hold sacred that you will be very careful."

"I will be very, very careful!" Kyril promised. "And now that I have told you my secret, tell me how you think you can prevent the King from proposing to Stephanie, with Cousin Augustina putting the words into his mouth and doubtless holding a pistol to his head."

"I cannot tell you that," Laetitia said, "not because I wish to be secretive, but because, although I have a plan forming in my brain, it is not yet complete . . . and, Kyril, I am terribly afraid of failing!"

Even as she spoke she thought of the *Voivode* and could almost hear him saying:

"The way will be shown to you."

It was impossible to put into words what she was feeling, but she said again:

"Just trust me, and pray, pray hard that I will be successful."

Kyril put his arms round her and kissed her.

Then, as if he could not bear to talk about it any more, he walked from the Drawing-Room and she heard him going into the small kitchen to find Gertrude.

* * *

Laetitia looked at the clock and knew she still had an hour before dinner.

This meant she just had time to speak to Stephanie alone, because the Grand Duke and Grand Duchess would be in their bedrooms and Stephanie would be in hers.

The Grand Duchess always insisted that meals should be served with great pomp and ceremony, as they had been in her father's Palace.

The Grand Duke's father, on the other hand, when the family was alone had preferred informal meals at which there was no protocol, no Ladies-in-Waiting, and he could laugh with his wife and children.

And he knew that what was said at the table would not be repeated all over the Palace.

That was the way the present Grand Duke had been brought up, and when he married he had at first protested at the long-drawn-out formal meals with a servant behind every chair and the presence of *Aides-de-Camp* and Ladies-in-Waiting, which inevitably restricted their conversation.

But as always the Grand Duchess had her own way,

and she even insisted on wearing a tiara every night and
that the Grand Duke should put on his decorations.

"It is so deadly boring," Prince Paul had often complained, "that in the future I shall make every excuse not to
go to the Palace unless I absolutely have to."

But because he loved his cousin Louis, when the
Grand Duke pleaded with him he could not refuse.

Laetitia remembered how he would grumble when he
had to put on his silk stockings and knee-breeches and wear
his ribbon of the Order of St. Michael across his white shirt
and the glittering crosses on his evening-coat.

"You look very smart, Papa," she would say when he
came downstairs to where the carriage was waiting outside
the door of their house.

"If you want to know the truth, I am damned uncomfortable," her father replied.

This made her mother exclaim:

"Really, Paul, you must not swear in front of the
children!"

"They would swear if they were in my shoes," Prince
Paul replied and laughed.

Then as he reached the Hall he would look at his wife
with her tiara of sapphires and diamonds on her head and
the same stones round her neck and say:

"The only consolation I have is that you look lovely,
darling, and the only mistake is that you should be a Grand
Duchess, rather than a certain lady whose name we must
not mention in front of the children."

Marie-Henriette, who was quite small at the time, had
clapped her hands and said:

"I know who you mean—Cousin Augustina! She is
horrible and always tells me to shut up and go away."

"Now you see what you have done?" Princess Olga
exclaimed.

But Prince Paul only laughed.

"One cannot hide the truth," he said, "and I repeat,
my darling, you should be a Grand Duchess or, better still,
a Queen!"

He kissed his wife, and as he turned towards the door
he said:

"Good-bye, children! I would much rather be here with you than have to go to the Palace. But tomorrow, to make up for my discomfort, we will have a picnic in the garden and wear our oldest clothes."

They would all cheer and wave as their father and mother drove away, then they would start to chatter excitedly about what they would do the next evening.

'We were so happy then,' Laetitia thought as she let herself out the front door.

Then she went through the gate which led into the Palace garden and, just as Stephanie had done, hurried through the bushes until she reached the side of the Palace where there were no guards.

She was hoping fervently that the side-door would not be locked, and to her relief she was able to let herself in without anybody being aware of it.

Then, going up the back-staircases used only by the servants, she reached Stephanie's bedroom without being seen by anybody.

She entered it and found, as she had hoped, that Stephanie was alone there except for her lady's-maid.

As she walked in, Stephanie gave an exclamation of pleasure.

"Laetitia, how lovely to see you!" she said. "I was wondering how I could get in touch with you."

Laetitia knew the reason was that she wanted to hear if Kyril had arrived, and as she kissed her cousin she said:

"I have a lot to tell you."

Stephanie looked at her maid.

"Wait outside, Dorothya," she said, "and warn us if anybody is coming. I want to talk to Her Highness and no-one must know she is here."

Dorothya, who had been with Stephanie for years, smiled at Laetitia,

"It's nice to see Your Highness," she said, "and I hope your honourable mother is well."

"Quite well, thank you, Dorothya," Laetitia replied.

The maid curtseyed, then went through the door and shut it behind her.

"Quickly, tell me what you have to say," Stephanie

said in a conspiratorial whisper. "And if by any chance Dorothya warns us that Mama is approaching, you must hide in the wardrobe."

Laetitia knew she must be as quick as possible, and she therefore said without wasting time:

"Kyril is back and is longing to see you. He says he will meet you at your usual place tonight."

Stephanie's eyes lit up with excitement, and she looked so pretty that it flashed through Laetitia's mind that anybody would know she was in love.

"Now listen, Stephanie," she said, "I have warned Kyril that he must be very, very careful and that it would be disastrous if your mother had any idea of what you felt for each other."

"I know that."

"Mama told me today that she is sure that if Cousin Augustina suspected that you were in love with Kyril, he would be sent to the Prussian Army Training School."

Stephanie gave a loud cry.

"How could I bear that to happen to him? I know Papa thinks it is a ghastly place."

"I think it would destroy Kyril," Laetitia said. "So, Stephanie, do remember that you must hide your feelings. I really think it would be best not to protest when your mother says you are to marry the King!"

She saw Stephanie shiver as she said:

"I cannot . . . marry him! I will . . . not! Oh, Laetitia what am . . . I to do?"

It was a cry that Laetitia had heard so often before that she merely said quickly:

"Do not think about it! Forget it for the moment, and just be happy because Kyril is back."

"You promised to help me and prevent the King from proposing to me."

"That is what I am trying to do."

"But we have only two more days. He will be here on Wednesday."

"Yes, I know," Laetitia said, "but please, Stephanie, for the moment just think and pray that it will not be as bad as you anticipate. At the same time, remember that you and Kyril, if you meet secretly, are doing something that is very, very dangerous."

"I promise I will remember," Stephanie replied, "and I am praying, Laetitia, as you told me to do, praying for hours every night and every moment of the day that Kyril and I can be together."

"Just go on praying," Laetitia said, "and somehow a miracle will happen and your wish will come true."

Stephanie's face lit up again. Then she put her arms round Laetitia and kissed her.

"I love you!" she said. "All I want is to be your sister-in-law."

The way she spoke brought a lump to Laetitia's throat. Then she said:

"I must go! If anybody tells your mother I am here she might be suspicious."

"No-one saw you arrive?" Stephanie asked anxiously.

"I do not think so," Laetitia replied, "but in this place the walls have eyes as well as ears!"

As she spoke, she knew that Stephanie was not listening.

"If I am going to see Kyril," she said, "I am going to put on one of my prettiest gowns."

"If you are going to change you had better hurry," Laetitia replied. "It would be a mistake to be late for dinner and annoy your mother."

"Yes, of course."

Laetitia opened the door.

Dorothya was outside, keeping guard.

"Thank you, Dorothya," Laetitia said softly as she passed her.

Dorothya dropped her a little curtsey and went back into the bedroom, and Laetitia crept down the stairs.

She reached the garden-door, and the only danger now was that she might be seen when she crossed into the bushes.

Fortunately, very few rooms on that side of the Palace were occupied, and she moved quickly.

She did not look back, hoping that if anybody saw her they would think she was one of the servants having perhaps an illicit meeting with one of the gardeners or sentries.

When she was out of sight of the highest windows in the Palace, she ran, and by the time she reached the courtyard and their own front door she was breathless.

She entered the house to find Kyril waiting for her.

"It is all right," she gasped, "I have seen her and she is very excited at the thought of seeing you again."

"You warned her to be careful?"

"Yes, of course, and she knows even better than we do how vindictive Cousin Augustina would be if she had the slightest suspicion that there is anything new in your relationship."

Kyril gave a sigh of relief.

He had had his bath and was in his shirt-sleeves.

He put his arms round his sister and hugged her.

"Thank you, dearest of sisters," he said. "I had no right to ask you to go into the lion's den, but I am very grateful."

'The lion's den' was an apt description, Laetitia thought when she reached her own room.

At the same time, the Grand Duchess was even more dangerous than any lion could be.

Laetitia knew she would be increasingly worried all the time Kyril was at home in case, through one indiscreet word or one intercepted look, the Grand Duchess should become suspicious.

"Please, God, keep him safe," she prayed.

She was still praying when the evening, which had been one of laughter and happiness, was over.

When Kyril had said he was retiring to bed early, she knew exactly where he was going, and she only hoped that her mother had no idea of it.

She heard him slip out of the house and knew he was making his way as she had done through the bushes towards the Palace.

There was a moon that night, and she knew that if he was not careful it would be easy for anyone to see him climbing the walls of the Palace, and he might even be shot by a zealous sentry.

Then she told herself reassuringly that nothing ever happened in Ovenstadt.

As far as she knew, there were no revolutionaries or trouble-makers like those whom Princess Aspasia had described in Zvotana, and in consequence those who guarded the Grand Duke had become very slack.

When they were not expecting to be observed, the sentries on the gates would talk to one another or even lean against the railings and put down their rifles instead of carrying them on their shoulders.

They would also chat good-humouredly to anyone going in or out, and because they knew Laetitia and Marie-Henriette, they were disappointed when they did not stop to gossip.

Last week they had wanted to talk about the King's visit and the Regiments which were being recalled to the Capital to line the route and provide an impressive Guard of Honour when His Majesty arrived.

"That means a lot of 'spit and polish' for us, Your Highness," one of the sentries complained. "We're kept at it night an' day."

"Think how smart you will look," Laetitia said, "and how much the girls will be admiring you."

"As long as my girl don't admire anyone more than me, 'twill be all right!" the sentry answered. "I don't fancy too much competition."

Laetitia had laughed at him, and when she had gone on to the front of the Palace with a note from her mother accepting an invitation she had received for the State Luncheon and the Ball, she thought it was undoubtedly the sort of conversation the Grand Duchess would have frowned upon.

As they had expected, they had received only the minimum number of invitations to which as a family they had a right.

Princess Olga had been invited to the luncheon which would be given immediately upon the King's arrival, but Laetitia and Marie-Henriette were excluded from that and had been invited only to the State Ball.

Marie-Henriette could think of nothing but what she

was to wear, and besides working on her Gypsy dress Laetitia had been doing everything possible to alter and make the gowns they had worn for years appear new and attractive.

"If only I could give you one of my dresses," Stephanie had said when she found them working busily in the Dining-Room because it was easier to put their things on the table.

"I wish you could!" Marie-Henriette replied. "Whatever I do with this gown, it is still going to look dowdy and out of fashion."

"Mama would kill me if she thought I had given away anything without . . . asking her," Stephanie said unhappily.

Then as she looked at the frills on Laetitia's gown, which looked after several years of wear rather crushed and limp, she exclaimed:

"I have an idea!"

"What is it?" Marie-Henriette asked.

"Last year Mama bought two rolls of tulle intending to have both of them made into gowns for me. Then the woman who works in the Palace was taken ill and I think she forgot about them."

Marie-Henriette looked excited.

"Some nice stiff tulle is just what I want to put round the hem of my gown, and it would make all the difference to Laetitia's frills."

"I am sure no one will notice if they disappear from the cupboard outside on my landing," Stephanie said. "One roll is white and the other a very pale blue, just the colour of your eyes, Hettie."

Marie-Henriette clasped her hands together.

"Oh, please, please, Stephanie, be brave and give them to us!"

"I will," Stephanie said. "I will send Dorothya with them as soon as I get back to the Palace."

She kept her word, and Dorothya had arrived an hour later with a washing-basket in her arms, in which under an old piece of cloth the rolls of tulle were hidden.

They were exactly what Laetitia thought she needed to

stiffen the frills of her gown and give it an attractive, fairy-like look, very suitable for a débutante.

There was also enough tulle to drape round the bodice, and it really transformed her gown into something so elegant that she knew, King or no King, she would enjoy the Ball simply because she was looking her best.

Marie-Henriette was in raptures over what the blue tulle had done for her gown, which was of pale blue and had been made for her just before her father died.

As it was, it had looked too young and not sophisticated enough for a girl of nearly seventeen.

"I am going to transform it into a gown which will look as if it is a model straight from Paris!" she cried.

She attached two frills of the tulle round the hem, which made it just the right length, and with frills to match over her shoulders and round the low neck, she looked very lovely.

When she put it on, Laetitia felt that if there was the handsome Prince they both prayed for at the Ball, he would certainly fall in love with Hettie.

It was fortunate that she had almost finished her Gypsy dress by the time Stephanie produced the tulle, and when they were not with Kyril, who actually could spend very little time at home, they worked until their Ball-gowns were ready.

'What would be disastrous now,' Laetitia thought, 'would be if Cousin Augustina finds out about Stephanie and Kyril, and then we all shall be banned from going to the Palace!'

Then she told herself that it was unlucky even to think such things, and instead she prepared very carefully what she could say to her mother about what she intended to do tomorrow.

She waited until they were going to bed, then she said:

"Mama, I never told you I had a message today from *Fräulein* Sobieski."

"A message, dearest?" the Princess enquired.

"Yes, she begs me to come to see her. I do not think she is very well, and you know how old she is."

Fräulein Sobieski was one of the first Governesses

whom she and Marie-Henriette had ever had, and when she retired she went to live in a cottage which was not far from Thor Castle.

She lived there alone, and whenever Laetitia could spare the time she would ride over to see her and spend a few hours with her old Governess.

"What I thought I would do, Mama, if you agree," Laetitia said now, "is to ride to see *Fräulein* Sobieski tomorrow. I could stay the night with her and come back early the next morning."

The Princess considered this for a moment before she said:

"I think that would be wiser than trying to do it all in one day. I would not want you to tire yourself before the festivities."

Laetitia smiled.

"We shall watch the festivities from the roadside!" she said. "We are not asked for the luncheon, as you have been, on the first day, so we will watch the King inspect the Guard of Honour, and then we will come back here and eat bread and cheese while you are enjoying an exotic menu in the Grand Dining-Hall!"

The Princess laughed.

"You are making yourself out to be poor little 'Cinderella,' but I would willingly change places with you. You know how heavy and pompous those luncheon-parties are."

Laetitia laughed.

"Hettie and I are determined to cheer up the Ball, if nothing else, and I expect before that we shall be able to hide upstairs and hear from Stephanie what is happening."

"Cousin Augustina will not like that, if she hears about it," the Princess said quickly.

"We will keep out of her way," Laetitia promised, "but you know, Mama, we have to keep impressing on Stephanie how careful she must be not to make Cousin Augustina suspicious."

"I cannot bear to talk about it," the Princess said. "It makes me so frightened! Kyril has promised to be very discreet, and of course he has not been invited to anything except the Ball."

Laetitia knew her mother had no idea that Kyril and Stephanie were meeting secretly, and she thought it wiser not to tell her.

Instead she kissed her and said:

"Try not to worry, Mama, and I will give your love to *Fräulein*. You know how much she adores you."

"You must take her a present, dearest," the Princess said. "I am sure I have something she would cherish."

It was so like her mother to want to give presents when she had so little herself, and Laetitia said quickly:

"I will find something, Mama."

She said good-night and went to her room, thinking that what she had dreaded had passed off better than she expected.

She had already packed her Gypsy dress very carefully in a rolled-up cloth that she could attach to *Kaho*'s saddle.

She had also warned Kyril that in no circumstances was he to take *Kaho* if he wanted to ride.

"I prefer him to *Chino*," he said quickly.

"I daresay, but I have to go quite a long way for what I intend to do, and as *Kaho* is more reliable, you will have to leave him for me."

The way she spoke made Kyril realise that what she was planning concerned him, and he said quickly:

"You must tell me, Laetitia, what you are up to. I will not have you taking any risks on my behalf."

"I am not going to tell you," Laetitia replied, "simply because I am not quite certain myself, and I shall have to play it by ear. What I want you to do is to *will* me to be successful."

Kyril's eyes twinkled as he said:

"I have a feeling, on hearing that expression, that you are using Gypsy magic. I know they believe it is their will as well as their charms which can make a spell effective."

"Papa always believed that if we wanted something badly enough, we could get it," Laetitia said. "He told me that when he wanted to marry Mama and everybody said it was impossible, he willed it by sending out what he described as 'flashes of lightning'! Because they came from his heart and were so strong, he was confident that they would obtain for him what he wanted."

"Well, he certainly got Mama!" Kyril conceded.

"She was doing the same thing, and Papa said the force between the two of them was irresistible."

"Is that what you are doing now?"

"Exactly! And what I want you to do is to send out the flashes of lightning, as Papa called them. Tell the fates or God, if you like, that Stephanie must be yours, and with the help of the Gypsies it should work."

"What I think you are about to do frightens me," Kyril said. "Promise me, Laetitia, that you are not doing anything which might harm you in any way."

The anxiety in his voice told Laetitia how much he loved her, and she said:

"You know, dearest, I would do anything, however difficult, if it would make you happy. However, I promise you that what I am planning is not really reprehensible, only, shall I say, slightly daring and unconventional."

"Tell me," Kyril pleaded.

She shook her head.

"I do not want to talk about it. Just will, and go on willing, and I feel convinced in my own mind that somehow, while undoubtedly it is going to be a battle, we shall win!"

Chapter Four

*R*iding away on *Kaho*, Laetitia thought that so far everything had gone smoothly.

She had not left early, which meant she had had time to see Kyril at breakfast. Then, when he left, Stephanie arrived with a note which was to be given to him secretly.

"I cannot stop," she said. "Mama is rampaging all over the Palace, polishing everything in sight for the King, who I doubt will even notice, although she is sure he will."

Laetitia knew what the Grand Duchess was like when she was in one of her periodical cleaning moods.

The housemaids were sent scattering here, there, and everywhere, and the Housekeeper was scolded for not having everything so spotless that the Grand Duchess could run a silk handkerchief over it and not find a speck of dust.

It was something that happened fairly regularly in the spring and usually reduced half the Palace staff to tears.

"Did Kyril get home quite safely?" Stephanie asked in a whisper when she was alone with Laetitia.

"He was here for breakfast," Laetitia answered, "but, Stephanie, you must not let him take such risks too often. You know as well as I do what would happen if you were discovered."

"I know, I know!" Stephanie said miserably. "But I cannot stop thinking that if you do not save me I shall have

66

to . . . marry the King and never . . . see Kyril . . . again!"

Tears came into her eyes, as they had before, and Laetitia said hastily:

"Go back to the Palace now. If Cousin Augustina thinks you are here because of Kyril, she might become suspicious."

The idea frightened Stephanie so much that she kissed Laetitia quickly, then ran away, looking like a small animal that was being hunted.

Once again Laetitia sent up a prayer that she would be successful in saving Stephanie and Kyril from such unhappiness and went up to her mother's room.

Princess Olga did not rise early in the morning, because the girls insisted that she should have breakfast in bed.

They took turns in carrying it upstairs after Gertrude had prepared it, and now the Princess was sitting up in bed, looking very pretty and very much younger than she actually was.

"Good-morning, dearest," she said. "If you are off to see *Fräulein*, I hope you have found something to take her."

"Yes, I have, Mama. A scarf which Stephanie gave me at Christmas," Laetitia said, "and which I have never worn, and I also have a sketch drawn by Hettie of Kyril. It is not very good, but I know *Fräulein* will like it."

"I am sure she will," Princess Olga replied, "and, dearest, ride carefully and do not be late back tomorrow morning, or I shall be worried."

"I will be back very early," Laetitia promised.

She bent and kissed her mother. Then as she went to the door her mother said:

"Gustave will look after you. He is such a kind little man."

Laetitia did not reply, hoping that later when her mother found that Gustave had not accompanied her she would think she had not heard what she had said.

Instead, she hurried to the stables where Gustave had *Kaho* ready for her.

She had already given him her clothes, which were now attached at the back of her saddle, making it look rather strange when she was mounted on *Kaho*.

But there was no-one to see her and there was no other way of conveying her dress and what she would want for the night.

Gustave tightened a girth, and as he did so Laetitia said:

"Her Highness thinks you are accompanying me, Gustave, so do not let her see you unless you can help it. If she does, tell her you thought Prince Kyril wanted to ride *Chino*."

Gustave, who was well versed in the somewhat tortuous manner in which Laetitia got her own way, grinned.

"I've got to go down to the shops, anyway," he said. "After that I'll keep out of Her Highness's way, and her won't have a sight or sign of I."

"Thank you, Gustave," Laetitia said gratefully and rode off.

It was a lovely day with a touch of wind which kept it from being too hot.

The birds were singing, the butterflies hovering over the flowers, and it seemed almost impossible that everything should not be right with the world.

But Laetitia knew she was feeling distinctly apprehensive, and only the *Voivode*'s words repeating in her mind kept a small flame of hope burning brightly.

By road it was over four hours' drive to Thor Castle, but over land by the direct route Laetitia knew it would take her little more than two.

However, she had to stop at *Fräulein* Sobieski's cottage on the way, and when she arrived in the small hamlet in which it was situated, she was then only about half-an-hour from the Castle itself.

Her old Governess's cottage was in one of the small villages built at the foot of the range of mountains where the Castle was situated and was sheltered by fir trees.

It was very picturesque, and the cottages with their white walls and red tiled roofs had always seemed to

Laetitia to fit into the landscape as if they were part of a fairy-tale.

The cottage to which *Fräulein* Sobieski had retired was a little larger than some of the others and had a small garden in front, which was bright with flowers.

Laetitia dismounted, tied *Kaho*'s bridle to the wooden fence, and walked up the crazy paving between the flower-beds to knock on the door.

She could hear her old Governess push back her chair over the flagged floor and come slowly, limping a little, to see who was there.

When she opened the door she gave an exclamation of surprise.

"Laetitia! My dear, I did not expect you!"

"I wanted to see you," Laetitia replied.

"You must be on your way to the Castle to meet King Viktor when he arrives this evening."

Laetitia did not contradict her, she merely walked into the small kitchen, which had been polished until it looked as clean as one of the brass saucepans hanging from the rafters.

"Tell me all about the family," *Fräulein* Sobieski said, "while I make you a cup of coffee."

As she busied herself at the stove, Laetitia told her about Kyril being home and the gowns that she and Marie-Henriette were refurbishing for the State Ball.

Only when *Fräulein* Sobieski set the coffee on the table in front of her did she say:

"I have brought you two small presents and I do hope you will like them."

"How very kind of you!" *Fräulein* Sobieski exclaimed. "I have heard how difficult things are for you all since your father died, and I know you have to account for every penny."

"How do you know that?" Laetitia enquired.

"I am afraid, my dear, I listen to gossip," *Fräulein* replied, "and everybody who comes here from the City talks about the way your dear mother is treated by the Grand Duchess."

"I had no idea it was common knowledge!"

Fräulein looked at her for a moment. Then she said:

"You must forgive me if I am telling you things that I should perhaps keep to myself, but your father and mother were always very kind to me when I lived with you, and I cannot bear to think you are not as happy now as you were then."

Laetitia felt there was no point in pretending when *Fräulein* Sobieski knew so much.

She therefore told her how strongly the Grand Duchess disliked them and how they were excluded in every possible way from the Palace and from taking part in any social entertainments.

"It is cruel! Cruel!" *Fräulein* exclaimed angrily. "But it is exactly what I have heard from so many people who all loved your father and, if they had the chance, would love you too."

Laetitia gave a little sigh.

"There is nothing we can do," she said, "except, as you used to say when I hurt myself, 'grin and bear it'!"

Fräulein Sobieski laughed.

"You were a very adventurous little girl, always falling out of trees or downstairs! I used to expect every day that you would break a bone in some way or another."

Laetitia thought she was being more adventurous than ever at the moment, and even if she did not break any bones, she might well get hurt. But that was something she could not tell *Fräulein*.

When she had finished her coffee she said:

"I was wondering whether you would mind if I stay here with you until this afternoon. I do not want to arrive too early at where I am going."

Fräulein Sobieski was delighted.

"Of course, dearest child," she said, "and you can put your horse in the stable at the back of the cottage. It is really only a small shed, but he will be safe there."

Laetitia did as she suggested, and when she returned *Fräulein* had luncheon ready for her.

It consisted of an omelette made with eggs from the few fowls she kept in a pen in the back garden, fresh vegetables, a little cream cheese which she had made herself, and some strawberries. Laetitia found it all delicious.

They talked about the old days, and time flew by until Laetitia said good-bye.

But before she left she found that *Fräulein* Sobieski was able to give her some information which she had been eager to discover.

"I hear," the old Governess said, "that the King has asked for there to be as little formality as possible on his arrival tonight."

Laetitia listened intently as she went on:

"The son of one of the families in the village works for Prince Cloviky, who, as you know, owns all the land in this part of Ovenstadt. He tells me the Prince will greet His Majesty when he arrives at the Castle."

Laetitia knew Prince Cloviky by name, and she remembered that he was an old man who had a very fine ancestral Castle, but it was too far away to be of use on this occasion as the King would obviously wish to reach the Palace as quickly as possible.

"With the Prince," *Fräulein* Sobieski went on, "will be the Lord Chancellor to represent the Government. The Prime Minister will be at the Palace tomorrow with the Grand Duke."

"And the Grand Duchess!" Laetitia finished. "It is she who has arranged for the King to come to Ovenstadt."

"I had heard that," *Fräulein* said, "and I suspect that as he is unmarried, Her Royal Highness hopes he might propose marriage to Princess Stephanie."

Laetitia was not surprised that she should know this, because it was obvious that the Grand Duchess's ambitions would not have gone unnoticed.

"Do you think His Majesty would make Stephanie a good husband?" Laetitia asked deliberately.

"He is rather old for her," *Fräulein* replied, "and of course one hears stories that may or may not be true."

"What sort of stories?"

"I should not be repeating these things to you, but they say he is very attractive and the ladies find him irresistible."

"Is that because he is a man or because he is a King?" Laetitia asked.

"Kings naturally have a glamour all of their own," *Fräulein* said, "but after working in Royal Palaces all my life, I know that many of them are lonely and unhappy, and if what I am told is true, King Viktor is very cynical."

"Cynical?" Laetitia exclaimed. "Why should he be that?"

"I have heard," *Fräulein* replied, "that he was crossed in love when he was young, and has never got over it."

This was something Laetitia had not expected.

"How interesting!" she exclaimed. "Do tell me more!"

"The person who told me this," *Fräulein* replied, "lives in Zvotana, but she sometimes comes to stay with me for a few days. She also was a Governess to one of the King's Royal relatives."

"So he was crossed in love!" Laetitia repeated as if to herself.

"My friend said that the girl on whom he had set his heart would not accept him because he had no prospects!"

She gave a laugh.

"She must be feeling rather silly now when he has unexpectedly become King of Zvotana."

"If she cared only for his position and not for him as himself," Laetitia said, "he is lucky to have lost her."

Fräulein smiled.

"I am glad, my dear, that you are just as romantic as you used to be. I have always hoped that you would not lose your ideals, and that someday you will find a husband as charming and as noble as your dear father."

"That is what I want," Laetitia said, "but God does not make many men like Papa."

"It would certainly be difficult to find another Prince Paul," *Fräulein* sighed, "but one never knows, and I hope that dear little Princess Stephanie, whomever she marries, will be happy."

"So do I," Laetitia said fervently, and sent up a little prayer that it might be Kyril.

* * *

When the heat of the day had passed and the shadows

grew a little longer, she said good-bye to *Fräulein* Sobieski and, resaddling *Kaho*, set off again in the direction of the Castle.

As she drew near to it she thought it looked very magnificent standing high above the valley with the mountains behind it.

There was a road leading up to it which zig-zagged to make the gradient easier for the horses, and as she looked at it she saw that only a hundred feet below the Castle itself was what she had prayed would be there.

It was a Gypsy encampment set up on a flat piece of ground which had always been used by different tribes in the past.

It was a small plateau with steep cliffs above and below it, and it had been a resting place for the Gypsies for many generations.

Now bringing *Kaho* to a standstill, Laetitia could see the brightly coloured caravans where they had moved off the winding road and onto the level grass.

They were arranged in a half-circle, leaving a large space in the middle where she knew they would light their fire later in the evening.

It was then that they played their violins, and she remembered how their wild, enchanting melodies would rise up towards the Castle so that those inside would listen and feel thrilled by what they heard.

Some years ago, when they arrived on a visit to the Castle, there had been no Gypsies to be seen.

It had not been their winter visit, when it would have been impossible for the Gypsies to camp in the mountains, but it was spring.

So, both she and Kyril had been disappointed when they had ridden up the winding road to find the plateau empty.

Then when they had nearly finished dinner her mother had suddenly put up her hand and exclaimed:

"Listen!"

It was then that they heard the music of the violins, and Kyril had exclaimed with a light in his eyes:

"The Gypsies! I thought they would not let us down."

When dinner was over they had gone out onto the terrace from which there was a breathtaking panoramic view over the valley.

Just below them they could see the Gypsy fire glowing, and the music of the strings, the clash of cymbals, and the bell-like ring of tambourines filled their ears.

It had made Laetitia want to dance, and a few minutes later she, Kyril, and Marie-Henriette had flung open the windows and were dancing on the polished floor of the Baronial Hall.

Afterwards her father had sent money down to the Gypsies, and when they received it they stood waving to him.

Then they played a serenade, followed by a folk-song which was identified with the Regiment in which Prince Paul had served.

It had all been very moving, and Laetitia had thought then, as she thought now, that the Gypsies were their friends and no-one, not even the Grand Duchess, could prevent her from loving them.

She rode *Kaho* forward along the winding road until she could turn off it into the Gypsy camp.

The *Voivode* was there waiting for her, and she was sure that some of the younger Gypsies with their keen eyes had been watching her approach.

She greeted him and left *Kaho* in the charge of the boys who she knew would take good care of such a fine horse.

"I have everything ready, as Your Highness wishes," the *Voivode* said.

"You are very kind," Laetitia replied in Romany.

He smiled and drew her to a very prettily painted caravan that was next to his own.

"This is yours," he said, "for as long as Your Highness is gracious enough to use it."

Laetitia thanked him again, then she climbed into the caravan to find it was as attractive inside as it was outside.

The walls were painted with flowers and birds, the small windows were curtained with brightly coloured material, and on the floor there was a hand-woven rug which could easily have graced the Palace.

One of the Gypsy women brought her bundle from the saddle of her horse, and Laetitia laid it on the bed and took out her Gypsy dress.

The woman exclaimed with delight when she saw it.

"It is very beautiful! The gracious lady will look like one of us when she wears it, or perhaps more like one of our Russian sisters!"

"That is how I want to look," Laetitia exclaimed, "like a dancer!"

She had brought with her every petticoat she possessed to wear under a full skirt.

Fortunately, they had been bought in the days when her family was not so poor, and each one of them had a frill of deep lace which was very attractive.

Laetitia took off her riding-habit, and then with the help of the Gypsy woman she put on the petticoats, the blouse with its full sleeves, and the red silk skirt on which she had sewn innumerable glittering sequins.

Finally the black corset encircled her tiny waist, and when the Gypsy woman had laced it up the front, it made her look very slim and elegant.

Then the Gypsy woman unpinned her hair, letting it fall over her shoulders.

She brushed it until each strand seemed so full of electricity that it had a life of its own.

She tied back the sides with red ribbons and covered Laetitia's head with the veil with the gold coins framing her white forehead.

Perhaps because she was excited at what she was about to do, or perhaps because the veil was very becoming, her eyes seemed enormous in her small face, and her skin looked dazzlingly white in contrast to the skin of the woman who was tending to her.

Finally there were two little red slippers to go on her feet, anklets ornamented with gold coins, and bracelets which matched them tied on her wrists.

Then the Gypsy woman stood back and clapped her hands.

"The gracious lady looks like one of us!"

"Are you sure?"

"And very beautiful! A Gypsy, but not Hungarian—Russian!"

"That is what I wanted," Laetitia murmured.

It had taken a long time to dress her, and when she stepped a little shyly from the caravan onto the ground, she found the *Voivode* waiting outside.

"His Majesty has arrived at the Castle," he said.

Because she had been so intent on dressing herself, for a moment Laetitia had almost forgotten about the King.

"He is at the Castle?" she asked.

"He was received by two gentlemen with three others in attendance. His Majesty kept with him only two of his own people."

Laetitia smiled.

That was what she had hoped. A small party at the Castle would make things easier.

"My boys have been watching," the *Voivode* went on, "and they say in a few minutes His Majesty will sit down to dinner."

Laetitia knew, although the *Voivode* did not say so, that Prince Cloviky would not stay at the Castle but would return home.

That meant he would leave early as it was a long drive, and after that the King would be alone.

She also knew that the Lord Chancellor very much disliked late nights, and as he would have a long day ahead of him at the Palace, he too would make every effort not to stay up late conversing with the King.

She thought everything was going exactly as she wanted. At the same time, she felt afraid.

She had not been aware that the *Voivode* was watching her face, but after a moment he said quietly:

"Fear is destructive. Believe and have confidence in yourself."

"That is what I am trying to have," Laetitia replied.

"If fate is kind, everything will be as you wish."

He spoke slowly and positively and did not wait for her reply, but drew her towards the fire which had been lighted, and she knew she was to join the Gypsies in their evening meal.

She and the *Voivode* had chairs to sit on, while the tribe sat on the ground, and they were waited on by the younger women.

What was in the stew Laetitia had no idea, but it was more delicious than anything she had tasted for a long time.

She knew of course that the Gypsies used fresh herbs with everything they ate, and she felt she could detect the flavour of some of them, but it was difficult to put a name to what not only was very appetising but smelt very fragrant. After the stew there was a sweetmeat made with honey.

Then as the daylight faded and the stars came out overhead and the moon began to rise in the sky, Laetitia rose to her feet.

The *Voivode* rose too, and she said to him:

"You will watch for my signal?"

"We will do exactly what Your Highness asked."

As she hesitated, he added:

"Our blessings go with you, and the magic you asked for is yours."

That was what she wanted to hear, and she gave him a little smile before she walked away with nobody taking any notice or staring at her curiously.

The Gypsies with their acute perception knew that that would have embarrassed her.

Only as she reached the end of the plateau and started to climb the steps roughly cut in the rock which led directly to the Castle overhead did she realise that coming behind her and protecting her was one of the Gypsy boys.

He did not speak, he did not encroach on her, but she knew that the *Voivode* had sent him to give her confidence.

The steps were steep and she took them slowly, and as she climbed higher she knew that if she slipped it would be a long fall to the ground.

When she reached the terrace onto which the windows of the Castle opened, she moved in the shadows round to the side of it and found a great clump of flowering bushes.

This, she knew, masked one of the secret ways into the

Castle, which they had all known as children and which had made the great building a perfect place for games of "Hide and Seek."

Thor Castle in the Middle Ages had been fortified against the enemies of Ovenstadt, and several times the Royal Family had been besieged there by marauding hordes who sought to kill them.

But always they had been victorious, and one of the reasons had been that while their enemies blockaded what they thought was the only entrance into the fortifications, there were in fact several secret passages leading into the Castle, which were known only to the Rulers of the day.

Now Laetitia pushed her way through the bushes and found the entrance she sought.

It took her a little time to pull away the ivy which covered the door before it opened easily, and she started to walk along a passage which she knew would lead her to one of the towers.

At first it was dark, and she put out her hands to support herself.

Then there was the light coming through the open arrow-slits through which the first defenders of the Castle had fired their arrows.

Now the steps, little damaged through the years, curved round and round and she climbed upwards until she knew she was level with the First Floor of the Castle, above the Banqueting-Hall and the Drawing-Room.

This was the floor where the King would sleep.

There was a bedroom with a magnificent curtained bed which either the Grand Duke, if he was with them, or their father had used.

Opening out of it was a very comfortable private Sitting-Room where as children they were not allowed to intrude unless they were invited to do so.

"I must have one place where I can read the newspapers in peace," her father had said half-jokingly. "The rest of the Castle is yours, but this room is mine."

They used to tease him about it and say he only went there to fall asleep when he was tired from their chatter.

Laetitia thought she could remember every chair and table and every painting that hung on the wall.

She knew too exactly where the catch in the panelling was which would let her into the room.

Now as she pressed it very gently and the panelling began to swing open, she heard a man's voice say:

"Is there anything else you require, Sir?"

"No, thank you," replied another man, who she was sure was the King. "I have some State Papers to read, and after that I shall go to bed."

"State Papers are often long-winded and incomprehensible, and you have a long day ahead of Your Majesty tomorrow."

"I am aware of that," the King replied, "but I promise you I will not bore myself more than is absolutely necessary."

They both laughed, and the man who had spoken first said:

"Good-night, Sir. It is very quiet here, so I do not think you will be disturbed."

There was the sound of a door shutting and then a few seconds later the faint rustle of paper.

Laetitia moved slowly and silently into the Sitting-Room through the opening in the panelling.

Because her father had complained of a draught coming from that corner of the room, saying that the arrow-slits in the tower let in the wind, her mother had placed a screen there.

It was a very pretty one made of ancient tapestries that had come from other parts of the Castle and were too old to be used in their entirety.

She had cleaned them, and had kept the best pieces and joined them together to cover the screen.

Laetitia had loved looking at it ever since she was a little girl, pointing out to Marie-Henriette the animals, the men riding on horseback, and the ladies with long pointed head-dresses.

Now, after drawing in her breath, she walked slowly round the screen and into the room.

It was lit, as she expected to find it, not with the

oil-lamps that were used in most parts of the Castle, but by candlelight, because her father had preferred it.

On each side of the fireplace, in which there was a fire burning because it could often be a little chilly at night, there were two huge, fat candles set in carved stands.

There were several silver sconces on the walls, in each of which there were two lighted candles, and there was another large one on the table at the side of the King, who was sitting reading the papers he held on his knee.

Laetitia did not speak, and for a moment he was not aware that she was there.

Then, as if instinctively he sensed her presence, he looked up and appeared for a moment to be frozen into immobility.

But if he was staring in surprise at her, she was also staring at him, and he was not in the least what she had expected.

To begin with, he was very much more attractive than she had anticipated, even allowing for his Gypsy blood, and not only his hair but his eyes were black.

His features were clear-cut, and he was, she thought, not only one of the most handsome men she had ever seen but also the most unusual.

There was something about him which made him look different from anybody else, and she was also aware that *Fräulein* Sobieski had been right in saying he was cynical.

There were lines running from his nose to the corners of his lips which made him appear disdainful.

When he spoke there was a dry, almost mocking note in his voice as he asked:

"Are you real or an apparition?"

"I am real," Laetitia replied.

"Then I can only assume," the King said, "that the hospitality of Thor Castle is somewhat different from what I expected!"

Now there was definitely a cynical note in his voice and a look in his dark eyes that Laetitia did not understand.

As she moved towards him she said:

"I am a Gypsy and therefore we are joined by our blood."

"That is something I am usually told is most regrettable!" the King remarked.

"That is what you may hear in Zvotana," Laetitia said, "but here I and other Gypsies are very proud of belonging to the Rom."

"Where do you come from?" the King asked. "And how could you get into the Castle without the sentries and those in attendance upon me being aware of it?"

"I would like to show Your Majesty where a tribe of Kalderash is camped," Laetitia said. "It is traditional for the Gypsies to shelter under the protection of the Castle's shade."

As she spoke she moved to the window.

It was closed, and she opened the casement, knowing it was the signal for which those below were waiting and watching.

By the time the King had risen from his chair and crossed the room to where she was standing, the first strains of the Gypsy violins were moving upwards.

Laetitia knew the tune they were playing, which was a love-song of invitation, yearning, and desire.

"So that is where you come from!" the King said. "What did you say is the name of the tribe?"

"The Kalderash."

There was a little pause, as if he was trying to remember what he knew about them, and she said quietly:

"The metal-workers, and also the makers of magic!"

She sensed he was interested and went on:

"Would Your Majesty be interested in seeing the magic we perform? And would you let me show you how we dance?"

"You are a dancer?" he asked.

She nodded.

"What is your name?"

There was just a little pause before Laetitia answered: "Saviya."

She felt him stiffen, almost as if he felt it was an insult that she should bear the same name as his great-grandmother. Then he asked:

"Do you realise that name has a special meaning for me?"

"Of course! And I am honoured to bear the same name as the greatest dancer our race has ever produced!"

She felt he was pleased at her praise and went on:

"I could never aspire to such fame, but I would be intensely proud if Your Majesty would allow me to dance for you and you . . . alone."

She turned from the window as she spoke, and now as she moved back towards the hearth-rug she was aware that the King was looking at her searchingly.

Then he said:

"You are very beautiful, Saviya, as I suppose a great number of men have told you."

There was again that cynicism in his voice, which she did not miss, and Laetitia said:

"I have, as it happens, met very few men outside the tribe. As Your Majesty may not know, the Gypsy women are very strictly protected, first by their fathers, then by their husbands."

"Are you telling me you are married?" he enquired.

Laetitia smiled.

"No."

"Then all I can think is that the men in your tribe have no eyes in their heads!"

He stared at her and said:

"Tell me about yourself. I am interested."

"The violins are calling us, Your Majesty."

"Very well," the King said. "We will talk later. I will come now and see you dance. I presume you wish me to come alone?"

"You need not be afraid. It is not your rank that will protect you where we are concerned, but your blood."

"I am finding this remarkably intriguing," the King said. "I have always avoided Gypsies because I have either been teased about my Gypsy blood, or else it has been spoken of as a great misfortune."

"Tonight I hope you will change your mind," Laetitia replied, "and understand how very fortunate you are to be the great-grandson of Saviya."

"I have always been told she was very beautiful," the King answered. "But I cannot believe she was more beautiful than you."

Laetitia gave him a little smile and a provocative glance from under her eye-lashes.

Then she moved towards the door, and as she went through it she said:

"I will take Your Majesty a secret way out of the Castle so that nobody will know that you have left it."

She felt that the King was amused and becoming more and more intrigued, and she took him down a staircase which brought them out onto the corner of the terrace.

Here there were marble steps down into the garden, and she led him down the way by which she had climbed up from the plateau.

All the while they were descending the stone steps, the King moving rather cautiously, the violins were playing, and as the music grew louder Laetitia could feel it seeping into her heart and making her feet feel restless.

Then they reached the last step and the *Voivode* was waiting for them, looking, Laetitia thought, even more magnificent than he had when she had left him.

Now round his neck there were more gold chains which sparkled with red stones which she was sure were rubies, and on his fingers there were huge rings of the same jewels.

"May I welcome Your Majesty not as a King but as one of the Roms," the *Voivode* said respectfully.

"I am delighted to join you," the King replied simply.

The two chairs on which the *Voivode* and Laetitia had sat for supper had now been replaced by two carved elbow-chairs which seemed almost like thrones.

There was also a rug for the King's feet and a table at his side on which stood one of the exquisitely decorated goblets from which Laetitia had drunk before.

She saw a Gypsy woman fill it with wine, and then as the King joined the *Voivode* in a toast, Laetitia felt a hand pulling her away.

It was the Gypsy woman who had helped her dress, and now without speaking she took off her red veil and replaced it with a head-dress of red ribbons ornamented with gold and precious stones.

She could see it sparkling even when they were still in shadow.

The Gypsy woman then clasped a necklace of gold coins round her neck and screwed onto her ears some huge ear-rings to match, which had gold coins interspersed with red stones which again Laetitia suspected were rubies.

While she was doing this the violins burst into the wild, joyous music of a Gypsy dance, and the younger women of the tribe began moving hand-in-hand round the fire.

Then as each one loosed herself from the ring, she began to dance, at first slowly and gracefully, then with movements quickening and growing wilder and more exaggerated.

At the same time, Laetitia knew without being told that the music was not for her, and she had to wait.

At last, as the dance finished and the dancers moved into the shadows, she knew this was her moment.

Now the music changed and was softer, more entrancing, sweet and tender, and as Laetitia moved forward towards the fire, the Gypsies began to sing.

It was a beguiling melody and their voices seemed to blend not only with the music but with the stars in the sky above them and the moonlight turning the mountains and the Castle to silver.

At first the sound was delicate and tinkled like silver bells, then it became wild, invigorating, and exciting, and to Laetitia it drew her heart from her body and she became one with it.

Quicker and quicker the rhythm rose, and quicker and quicker Laetitia danced.

Every movement, every pirouette, every step she made seemed to come naturally to her, so that she did not have to think, because her instinct told her what to do.

Then as the music grew even wilder, she leapt round the fire with an unbelievable grace until she seemed to be carried up into the air as she leapt over it not once but twice.

Then once again she was moving more slowly, and she felt that she was no longer dancing with her body but with her soul.

When it seemed that the intensity was too much to bear, the wild, throbbing violence of the music was replaced by a soft, sweet melody coming like the peace of a rainbow after a storm.

Then Laetitia, as if told by a voice that came from outside herself, stood poised beside the fire and raised her arms, her whole body glittering as if she were one with the flames.

Then as she threw her head back in ecstasy and looked up at the stars, it was as if she commanded all those who watched her to raise their eyes higher than themselves.

She was absolutely still until, as the music died away to nothing more than a whisper, she seemed to fade into the darkness and disappear.

For a moment there was complete and absolute silence, and the King, who had not moved since Laetitia had begun to dance, suddenly drew in his breath as if he had forgotten to breathe for a long time.

Only as the music started again very softly did he feel as if he came back to reality, and instinctively he drained his glass, which had been refilled without his being aware of it.

"I had no idea that Gypsy dancing could be so wonderful!" he said to the *Voivode*, as if he must break the silence. "I am sure Saviya is exceptional. There cannot be another dancer as good as she is!"

"If there is, I have yet to see her!" the *Voivode* replied.

The King was about to say: "She is wasted here," then thought it would sound rude.

Instead he said:

"I can hardly believe that I have not been dreaming."

The *Voivode* smiled.

"Tomorrow Your Majesty will tell yourself it was part of our magic, or perhaps the wine you drank, and you will not believe what you have seen and felt."

The King was silent.

He was thinking that the dancing he had just wit-

nessed had given him an emotional experience he had
never encountered before.

Although he had no wish to admit it, he was aware that
there was no need to put it into words because the *Voivode*
knew what he was feeling.

Feeling he had to try to come back to normal, he said:

"If that is magic, I need not tell you how much I have
enjoyed it! Please, show me some more."

"Does Your Majesty mean that?"

"Of course! I have always heard about Gypsy magic,
but I have never had the opportunity of encountering it
before."

"We have one very special magic in this tribe which I
think perhaps would interest Your Majesty, if you are not
afraid to take part in it."

"Afraid? Of course I am not afraid!" the King replied.

"You are sure of that?"

"Very sure!"

There was silence. Then the King said:

"Show it to me. It is something I am longing to see,
and I may never have this opportunity again."

The *Voivode* looked at him before he said quietly:

"The magic I am suggesting, and in which Your
Majesty might wish to take part, is the magic of a Gypsy
marriage!"

Chapter Five

There was silence for a moment as the King stared at the *Voivode* in surprise.

Then slowly, because she was shy, Laetitia came from the shadows to stand beside him.

She had taken off the jewelled wreath, the ear-rings, and the necklace she had worn for the dance, and replaced them with her own. She again had on her hair the red veil with the gold coins outlining her forehead.

But the effort of dancing so wildly had brought a flush to her cheeks and a sparkle to her eyes so that she seemed to glow almost as if within her there was a light which was part of the flames of the fire.

The King looked at her. Then he said to the *Voivode:*

"And whom do you suggest I marry?"

"Who else but Saviya? But let me first explain something to you both."

The way he spoke was so solemn that both the King and Laetitia looked at him enquiringly, and he went on:

"If you were of my tribe, the Kalderash, I could not perform the ceremony I am going to suggest to you."

"Does not Saviya belong to your tribe?" the King interrupted in surprise.

The *Voivode* shook his head.

"My tribe are all pure bred and their blood is mixed with no other tribe, but Your Majesty and Saviya are not wholly Rom. Nevertheless, you will be permitted to see, to hear, and to feel what is forbidden to *gorgios.*"

The King did not speak, but Laetitia, because she could not help it, gave a little murmur of excitement.

This was something she had always longed for but had thought she would never be permitted to see.

The Gypsies were, she knew, fanatically secretive about their magic, just as they never answered questions from outsiders or talked of what was known only to their own tribe.

She was almost certain that the King was not aware of how proud they were of their blood and how the purity of it must not be soiled by a union not only with a *gorgio* but not even with a member of any other tribe.

As if he knew what she was thinking, the *Voivode* looked at her with wisdom and understanding in his expression before he began to explain.

It was his Hungarian blood which made him speak not only eloquently but with the culture of a man who in his own way of life was born a King.

"A marriage which takes place between a pure Gypsy and his bride is sacred and lasts until they die," he said. "For the Kalderash it is a sacrament which would be shocking to break. To do so would mean expulsion from the tribe."

He paused, then went on quietly:

"But there is another ceremony, used not amongst the Kalderash but amongst many other tribes, especially those in Russia and France."

He glanced at the King as he spoke, as if he remembered that he had been living there. Then he continued:

"This is a marriage which is, to all intents, a gamble in which both the bride and bridegroom are under the direction of the gods."

The King and Laetitia were listening intently as the *Voivode* continued:

"The main part of the ceremony consists of breaking an earthenware vessel. The number of pieces it breaks into shows the days, the weeks, the months, and the years for which the bride and groom must remain faithful to the other."

His voice deepened as he said impressively:

"At the end of that period, the husband and wife are free to separate or to break another earthenware vessel."

As he finished speaking, Laetitia drew in her breath.

Now she understood how the *Voivode* was answering her plea for help.

If the King would acquiesce, he would be tied to her for the days that he was in Ovenstadt and therefore would not be able to propose to Stephanie.

The problem, she thought frantically, was that he might either refuse to take part in such a ceremony or treat it lightly as a joke.

As if her thoughts communicated themselves to the *Voivode*, he said to the King:

"I must warn Your Majesty that to break these ties of magic before the time apportioned by the gods would leave you vulnerable to the curses and ill fortune of which all Gypsies are afraid."

There was just a short hesitation before the King replied:

"You can trust me, as the great-grandson of a pure-bred Gypsy, to keep to the conditions the ceremony will impose upon me."

Laetitia felt her heart leap.

Then with a faint smile as if he too was well satisfied, the *Voivode* replied:

"If that is your wish, then Your Majesty shall see what no-one without Romany blood in them has seen or heard."

It was so exciting that Laetitia could only clasp her hands together.

Then the *Voivode* said:

"The marriage ceremony will now commence, but first, Your Majesty, it is customary for the bridegroom to buy the bride, and if you have a gold coin you must give it to me."

"I think for what you are offering me," the King replied, "one gold coin is very inadequate."

He did not say any more, but unpinned from the white uniform coat he was wearing one of his decorations.

It was a diamond star, and as he put it into the Voivode's hand, the fire-light glittered on it and it appeared to be alive.

"Now for the 'Loving Cup,'" the Voivode said.

One of the Gypsies placed in his hands a huge goblet three times the size of those Laetitia had seen before.

It was made of gold, fashioned with the same exquisite, ancient workmanship, and covered in precious stones of all colours.

The Voivode handed it first to the King, who drank from it, and then to Laetitia.

The wine was delicious and, she thought, even more unusual than the wine the Voivode had given her when she had first visited him.

It seemed to have the same effect, for she felt suddenly as if everything was beautiful and golden. What was more, she was acutely aware of what she knew was an emotional response to everything round her.

It was difficult to explain, but she felt as if the brilliance of the stars came nearer, the light from the fire grew more vivid, and the dark shadows like velvet encompassed and protected them.

"Tonight," the Voivode was saying, "because the union between you shall be the end rather than the beginning of the evening, we will start with the feast."

Another chair was brought and set down beside those in which the Voivode and the King had watched the dancing. Now Laetitia sat between the two men.

A low table with gold dishes as splendid as the goblets from which they drank was set in front of them.

It was difficult to know or to remember afterwards what they ate, but, as she had found before, every dish was original and had flavour that she had never tasted before.

While they were eating there was the music of the violins, and after a short while Gypsies came one at a time in front of them to perform magic tricks which Laetitia had never guessed they knew or imagined she would ever see.

One Gypsy conjured up doves apparently out of the

air. He lifted his arms and they flew towards him, perching on his head, on his hands, and at his feet.

He would give an order in a low voice and three of them would fly in the direction he chose. Then they returned to circle round him three times before he allowed them to settle on his arms.

One went far off to fetch a leaf from a tree, another to bring back a flower in its beak.

They did everything he asked of them. Then suddenly as he told them to go they were gone, and he was standing alone in front of the fire.

It was so clever and also so beautiful that Laetitia knew the King must be as spellbound as she was.

Then a Gypsy woman, gorgeously dressed, her arms weighed down with the jewelled bracelets that the Kalderash treasured, brought three wicker baskets which she set down in front of her.

She held an instrument like a flute to her lips, and from the baskets, as Laetitia anticipated, came three cobras.

They were magnificent and looked very dangerous as they raised themselves up, their forked tongues moving wickedly in and out, their eyes gleaming.

Then just as the birds had obeyed the Gypsy man, so now the cobras obeyed the notes of the music, and swaying rhythmically moved any way the Gypsy woman wished them to do, twisting themselves round and round her neck.

Finally, as she suddenly played a note that was sharp and authoritative, they slid back into their baskets.

After that there was a gypsy who could conjure up flowers out of the air, make a plant in a pot grow in front of their eyes, and when it had grown high above their heads, he showed them a bird sitting on her nest in the centre of it.

It may have been worked by hypnotism.

At the same time, if it was, it was so brilliantly done, so realistic, that it was hard to accept that what they were seeing was not reality, and the tree, the bird, and the man who had conjured it all up were not really there.

It seemed to Laetitia as if time passed in a flash, until

the feast was finished, the table was moved away from in front of them, and the *Voivode* rose to his feet.

It was then that one of the Gypsies set something down beside him which Laetitia saw was a bunch of twigs.

She was surprised at this, because she remembered her father had told her once that certain twigs picked from seven different trees were the most sacred symbol in a Gypsy marriage.

Just for a moment she was afraid that if the *Voivode* made the incantation over the twigs, snapped them one by one, and threw them to the winds, she would be married by the sacred Romany vows to the King until one of them died.

But the *Voivode* did not break the twigs. He put them on one side and took bread and salt from the stool on which they lay.

He put the salt on the bread and handed a small piece to the King, and another to Laetitia, saying:

"When you are tired of this bread and this salt, you will be tired of each other."

He turned to the King.

"Now, Your Majesty," he said, "give your piece of bread to Saviya and take hers, and you must both eat them."

They did as he said, and then in the *Voivode*'s hand appeared a small earthenware jug.

It was filled with water, and as the *Voivode* lifted it high in the air as if it was an offering to the gods, he said in Romany, which Laetitia understood:

"Direct your power onto this vessel, and onto this man and woman who are to be joined together as husband and wife for as long as you decree."

Then violently, using all his strength, he dashed the jug down onto the ground between them, and as it broke Laetitia held her breath.

She knew that the King would stay in Ovenstadt until after he had received the Freedom of the City, which would take place on Friday.

If tonight's ceremony made it impossible for him to propose to Stephanie for three days, he would before then have left, and when he was gone, the Grand Duchess would presumably accept that her ambitious plan had misfired.

For a moment, because she knew how vitally important it was, she could not force herself to look and count.

Then as she heard somebody murmur "*Semno*," which she knew meant "five," she looked on the ground to see that the vessel had broken into five pieces.

The *Voivode* bent down, picked up the handle and gave it to the King, and handed a small piece to Saviya.

"You are now joined to each other," he said, "in an unbreakable bond as decreed by the gods for five days, or for any multiple of five. Keep this piece, preserve it carefully, and only if you lose it before the time decreed by the gods will misery, loneliness, and ill-luck come upon you."

The way he spoke was very impressive, so much so that Laetitia felt herself shiver just in case the King did not believe, as she did, that it would actually happen.

Then the *Voivode* drew a jewelled knife from his waist, and he took the King's right hand in his and Laetitia's left.

He made a minute prick on the wrist of each of them, just enough to make a drop of blood appear on their skin.

Then he held their wrists together so that their blood mingled, before he bound them with a silk cord with three knots in it.

He did not speak, but Laetitia knew, because her father had told her, that one knot was for constancy, the second for fertility, and the third for a long life.

She thought that if the King understood that, he might be afraid that he was being tricked into a marriage that would last for longer than five days, which was all that was entailed by the breaking of the vessel.

Then the *Voivode* said, and his voice seemed to ring out in the silence as the music of the violins ceased and all the Gypsies stood listening:

"Go in peace and know that the gods have blessed you. You have seen the magic that only those of our blood are allowed to see. You also have between you the magic that is yours alone, the magic which comes from the heart—the magic of love!"

As he finished speaking, the Gypsy violins burst into a paean of praise and triumph that rang out in the darkness.

Then there was a Gypsy boy holding a lighted torch as he moved toward the cliffs.

After him went a man playing a violin, and the King and Laetitia without being told knew they had to follow.

As they went, moving past the fire, the Gypsies began to sing again one of their love-songs that was both soft and inviting, alluring and provocative, and at the same time moving, although it was a theme of triumph and fulfilment.

They reached the steps which rose from the plateau up towards the Castle and followed the torch of the boy guiding them.

It was only afterwards that Laetitia thought it strange that she and the King with their hands bound together had been able to climb side-by-side up the narrow steps.

They reached the top, the Gypsy still playing, and behind them the music from the foot of the cliffs joined with his.

A little farther on the boy with the torch stopped and stood waiting for them to pass him, the man with the violin bowing respectfully as they did so.

The King paused and said to him:

"Tell your *Voivode* that you are always welcome in Zvotana, and on my return I will make it law that the Gypsies shall never be persecuted or turned out of my country for as long as I remain on the throne."

Laetitia saw by the expression of gratification and joy on the Gypsy's face that he understood.

Impulsively he went down on one knee and kissed the King's hand, and then Laetitia and the King walked up the steps and onto the terrace.

She did not look back, knowing that the Gypsies thought it was bad luck to look back to a place they had left in case they should never return to it.

She drew the King through the secret entrance which led to the staircase by which they could reach the First Floor without being seen.

They walked up the stairs in silence and along the passage to the Sitting-Room which they had left many hours earlier.

Only when Laetitia saw the candles guttering low and the fire just a red glow amongst the ashes did she feel as if she had lived through a lifetime of emotion and it was hard to come back to reality.

Then she was shyly conscious that the King was holding her hand and they were bound together by the silken cord.

"Shall I . . . undo this?" she asked in a voice that did not sound like her own.

She did not wait for his reply but undid the cord, and only when she could take her hand from his, and was conscious that the tiny cut the *Voivode* had made with his knife was throbbing a little, did she look up at him.

She then realised that he was looking at her with his dark eyes in a way that made her vividly aware that they were alone.

"So we are married!" the King said quietly. "Which is it to be, Saviya? Five days, five weeks, or perhaps for an eternity?"

She was surprised at his question. Then she said quickly, thinking of Stephanie:

"I think Your Majesty will find that . . . five days is quite long enough, but please, you . . . must keep . . . it."

"I have given my word," the King replied, "and I never consciously break a promise."

Because that was what she wanted to hear, Laetitia said:

"I am glad . . . so very . . . glad you . . . feel like that."

"How could I feel anything else," the King asked, "when tonight has not only shown me things I never knew existed but has brought me you?"

As he spoke there was a sudden depth in his voice, and she thought there was a fire in his eyes that had not been there before, and she was aware for the first time that she was in danger.

She would have taken a step away from him, but it was too late.

His arms went round her, and as he pulled her to him he said:

"You are my wife, my Gypsy wife, whom fate or the gods have given to me."

Before she could even put up her hands to ward him off, his lips came down on hers.

Laetitia had never been kissed before, although she had thought about it, and she had always imagined it would be something soft, gentle, and in a way comforting.

But the King's lips were hard and possessive, and as he made hers captive, he hurt her.

Then even as she thought she must struggle and be free of him there was a strange magic.

It was what she had felt when she was dancing and which had been part of the happiness she had found after drinking the Gypsy wine.

It seemed to grow and intensify until she felt not only her lips grow soft and yielding but her whole body move as if to music.

Then the King's arms drew her closer and still closer to him.

A rapture and ecstasy like the flames of the fire within her breast rose from her throat into her lips.

She knew then that his kiss joined them by a far greater magic than anything they had received from the *Voivode*.

It was a magic that was not only part of her body but of her heart and her soul; a magic so vivid, so compelling, and at the same time so overwhelming that it was life itself.

The King's lips became very insistent and more possessive, and at the same time there was something that had not been there at first.

Laetitia felt vaguely at the back of her mind that it was almost as if he realised the sanctity of what had taken place, and that for the moment at any rate they were joined spiritually as well as physically.

He raised his head. Then he said hoarsely:

"How can you be so perfect and what I have been searching for all my life?"

Then he was kissing her again, kissing her wildly and triumphantly, echoing the music of the violins when they left the camp.

It had a magic that Laetitia felt swept her up towards the stars that were shining overhead.

Yet, at the same time, she knew that the flames of fire burning through her body came from a fire within the King.

They leapt higher and higher, and when Laetitia felt as if the sensations she was experiencing were so intense that it was almost impossible to breathe, he took his lips from hers to say:

"You are my wife! I want you, now at this moment, as I know you want me!"

For a moment she could hardly understand what he was saying.

Then, as if some modicum of sanity returned to her mind, she remembered that she was not Saviya, a Gypsy dancer. She was Princess Laetitia, her mother's daughter, and somehow she had to escape.

Then as if the magic of the evening overpowered everything else, she wanted the King to go on kissing her, and to be closer and still closer to him.

Wildly, inevitably, irrepressibly, she wanted him to love her and to give him her love in return.

It was as if every nerve in her body was crying out for him, responding to the closeness of him and of what he asked of her.

"I must . . . go! I . . . must go!" Laetitia told herself, but her whole being was crying out to stay.

It was impossible to leave the wonder of his lips, to ignore the fire which burned within them both.

The King was kissing her again, but not now on her lips.

Instead, his mouth moved over the softness of her neck, and it gave Laetitia a sensation she had never known before, which made her quiver against him, her breath coming quickly from between her lips.

"I . . . love . . . you!" she whispered. "I love . . . you . . . I love you!"

She was not certain whether she actually said the words or if they were whispered within her heart.

"And I love you, my beautiful bride!" the King replied. "Come, my darling, why should we waste time standing here?"

He drew her towards a door which Laetitia knew led into the bedroom her father had always used.

It was only then, when she thought of her father, that she knew if he were there he would stop her from doing what the King wanted.

As she thought of him, it was almost as if he were in the room, looking a little stern as he had when she behaved badly, and at the same time knowing what was best for her.

"It is . . . wrong," she said in her heart.

They had reached the door of the bedroom, and as the King pulled it open and Laetitia could see the big canopied bed inside, she knew she must escape and her father was telling her how to do so.

"Please," she said in a voice that was barely above a whisper, "could I have . . . something to . . . drink?"

The King smiled.

"Of course," he said. "I think the salt has made us both thirsty."

He took his arm away and leaving her walked towards the table which stood in a corner of the room.

Without looking, Laetitia knew there was always wine there for anybody who needed it.

She expected too, because it was a tradition of the Castle, that there would be a small jug of freshly made lemonade.

The King paused, looking at the array of decanters, bottles, and glasses.

"Wine, champagne, or lemonade! Which would you prefer?" he asked.

He waited for Laetitia to answer, and when there was only silence he turned round.

There was nobody in the room except himself!

* * *

Laetitia, having closed the secret panel in the wall very quietly, hurried down the twisting stairway of the tower and let herself out through the door which opened into the bushes.

Then she ran as quickly as she could to the top of the cliffs where the steps were.

As she reached them, she saw that sitting just below the top so that he could not be seen from the Castle windows was the Gypsy boy with the torch.

He rose as she appeared, and went down the steps ahead of her, holding the torch so that she could see where to put her feet.

She was looking down, concentrating on the steps, until she reached the ground, and only then did she look up.

To her amazement, the plateau was empty except for one caravan, the one she had used herself.

The Gypsy boy took her towards it, and now she saw that there was a horse between the shafts, and the Gypsy woman was waiting to help her out of her dress and into her riding-habit.

As she took off her velvet corset, something fell from it onto the floor of the caravan, and Laetitia saw it was the small piece of the earthenware jug.

She picked it up, and the Gypsy said:

"Keep it carefully, gracious Princess, it is very lucky."

"Yes, I know," Laetitia said with a smile.

"The *Voivode* left something else for Your Highness."

As she spoke, the Gypsy pointed and Laetitia saw lying on the bed beside her riding-habit the little bundle of twigs the *Voivode* had not broken at the wedding.

"Thank you," she said, trying to understand why they had been left for her.

With the Gypsy's help, it took only a few minutes to change her clothes, and when she was ready Laetitia said:

"Thank you, more than I can say. I wish I had something to give you to express my gratitude."

"There is no need, gracious Princess," the Gypsy woman replied. "My husband has told me of the King's promise that we shall be welcome in Zvotana. No gift could match what that means to us."

Laetitia knew that was true, because in so many countries the Gypsies were persecuted and imprisoned.

She therefore held out her hand, saying:

"Then I can only thank you from my heart."

The Gypsy curtseyed and kissed it, and then as Laetitia stepped out of the caravan she saw that *Kaho* was waiting for her.

The Gypsy boy tied her clothes onto the saddle and helped her mount.

Then as she rode away she heard the caravan moving after her across the plateau to join up with the rest of the tribe, who had already gone ahead.

She knew that after she and the King had gone back to the Castle they must have started off immediately, in order to avoid any embarrassing questions should he come in search of her.

"I do not expect he will bother to do that," Laetitia told herself.

And yet at the same time she thought he must be wanting her at this moment as she was wanting him.

Now that she had time to think, it was an agony that was hard to bear to know that she had run away.

His kisses and the emotions he had awakened in her were beyond anything she had ever imagined or dreamt of!

She longed for him and she wondered if he would regret that he would never again find Saviya—his Gypsy wife.

Because she could not help it, as *Kaho* came to the bottom of the twisting road which led up to the Castle she turned him round and looked back.

The Castle, now high above her with the mountains peaking behind it, appeared very strong and magnificent.

All the windows were in darkness except for one!

In that one the curtains were still drawn back and the window was open, as she had opened it to let in the music of the violins.

'What is he thinking now that he has found me gone?' she wondered.

Did he think that what had happened was all an illusion, part of the magic the Gypsies had promised him? That she had been just a mirage which he would soon forget?

The very idea was like the agony of a knife cutting into her, and she knew that what had been a piece of play-acting to save Stephanie had become something very much more serious to her.

She turned *Kaho* again and as she did so she was aware that the first fingers of the dawn were creeping up the sky and the stars were fading.

Dawn came quickly in Ovenstadt, and, as she had planned, she would be riding home in daylight.

But still she longed to stay, for she knew that whatever lay ahead, she had irrevocably left her heart in the Castle with the King.

* * *

Because *Kaho* was eager to get back to his own stall, he moved so fast that it was only a little after five o'clock when Laetitia saw the Palace just ahead of her.

She found it impossible to believe that so much had happened since she had left yesterday morning, desperately afraid that her plan would fail or that the *Voivode* would not do what she had asked of him.

She had simply begged him to use some magic on the King that would prevent him from asking for Stephanie's hand in marriage while he was in Ovenstadt.

"If His Majesty proposes while he is here on his State Visit," Laetitia had said, "the Grand Duchess will accept on the Princess's behalf, and it will be impossible for her to find a way of breaking the betrothal or to do anything but marry the King, whom she does not love."

She knew that to the Gypsies a betrothal between a man and a woman was almost as sacred as a marriage.

That the *Voivode* had responded in such a brilliantly clever fashion exceeded everything that Laetitia had expected of him.

At the same time, she herself had become involved in a way she had never anticipated.

She had known when she danced for the King—as she

had said, for him alone—that she had been transmitting her will in "flashes of lightning," as she had told Kyril to do.

She had been willing him to want her so that for the moment, at any rate, she could prevent him, with the help of Gypsy magic, from being interested in Stephanie.

She had thought it rather a forlorn hope, but miraculously he had responded.

What she had not envisaged was that she would be no less captivated and drawn to him than he had been to her.

"I want him! I want his kisses! I want his love!" Laetitia cried to herself, and was frightened at what such words implied.

There was no sign of Gustave so early in the morning, so she took *Kaho* into his stall, took off his saddle and bridle, and left him contentedly munching the food in his manger.

She slipped into the house by the back-door, creeping up to her bedroom so as not to disturb anybody, then undressed and got into bed.

As she laid her head on the pillow she thought that it would be impossible to sleep and she would lie awake thinking of the King, feeling again his lips holding hers captive, and recalling the wild sensations he had evoked when he kissed her neck.

She had known then what was meant by "the fire of love," and as she had felt it burn in her body, she knew it was very different from what she had expected, yet far more exciting, glorious, and ecstatic.

"How can I be in love with a man I have only seen for the first time today?" she asked herself.

Then she knew that when the King had looked up at her from his papers, she had felt he was different from any other man she had ever seen before.

It was fate that had sent her to him, or perhaps it was the gods who had been waiting to be invoked by the *Voivode* to decide how long their strange Gypsy marriage should last.

Then despairingly she asked herself what was the use of a marriage if they were not to be together and could not acknowledge themselves as man and wife.

She thought she must cry out at the misery of what she had lost.

Then all she could feel was the King kissing her, and the fire from his lips moving into her body and taking possession of her senses and her entire self.

"This is love!" Laetitia told herself.

It was a glory that seemed to fill the whole world and the sky, and it was impossible not to respond to it.

Chapter Six

L aetitia heard the door move quietly and opened her eyes.

For a moment she was still in her dreams, in which she was with the King.

Then she saw Marie-Henriette's face looking at her and came back to reality.

"You are awake!" Marie-Henriette exclaimed. "I thought you would sleep for another hundred years!"

With an effort Laetitia attempted to sit up in bed.

"What time is it?"

"After one o'clock, and Gertrude wondered if you wanted anything to eat."

"I do not believe it! How could I have slept for so long?"

"Mama said we were not to disturb you."

At the mention of her mother, Laetitia gave a little cry.

"The King! He has arrived?"

"Yes, I believe so," Marie-Henriette replied, "but Mama would not let us go and watch him inspect the Guard of Honour."

Laetitia pushed the hair back from her forehead.

"Why not?" she asked automatically.

"She said it was degrading for us to stand in the crowd when we ought to be waiting in the Palace to receive him."

Laetitia gave a little laugh.

"Cousin Augustina would never allow us to do that!"

"That is true," Marie-Henriette agreed, "but we will see him tonight at the Ball."

Laetitia felt as if she were coming back from another planet.

Because her thoughts had been so concentrated on the King and their Gypsy marriage last night, it was difficult to think of anything else.

She had almost forgotten the commotion that must be taking place in the Palace.

Now with a sudden lift of her heart she realised that unless anything went seriously wrong, she had saved Stephanie from receiving the proposal of marriage which the Grand Duchess had arranged.

As those thoughts swept into her mind, it made her feel quite weak, and she pressed herself back against her pillows.

"I will go fetch your breakfast," Marie-Henriette said. "You must be hungry."

Laetitia heard her running downstairs to the kitchen and told herself that all she had to concern herself with now was keeping out of the King's way at the Ball.

She was sure that because the Grand Duchess disliked them so much they would not be presented to him, and with over two hundred people in the Ball-Room it was very unlikely that he would notice her.

Her father had always said: "People see what they expect to see," and one thing was quite certain—the King would not expect to find his Gypsy bride as a débutante dancing in the Palace.

As she thought it over, she was convinced that her Gypsy disguise had been very effective.

All the time she had been with the King, both when they first met and afterwards when they had returned to the Castle and he had kissed her, she had been wearing the red veil with its decoration of gold coins on her forehead.

This meant that her black hair, which was so distinctive and very different from that of the other girls, was hidden.

It was true that when she had danced she had worn

instead the jewel-studded wreath from which flowed many brightly coloured ribbons. But they also had concealed her hair, and she had not been very near the King when she had danced, leapt over the fire, and then disappeared into the shadows.

"He will never recognise me," she told herself confidently.

And yet, at the same time, something irrepressible within her heart longed for him to do so.

How could she ever forget the rapture and ecstasy of his kisses?

She would always remember the way in which he had held her closer and closer to him until she had felt her body melting into his, and the wild sensations he had aroused in her when he had kissed her neck.

"I love him!" she whispered.

Then as she heard her sister coming up the stairs again, she told herself that the dream and the magic were over, and she had to behave correctly, as her mother and father would expect her to do.

Marie-Henriette put the tray down beside Laetitia. Then, sitting on the bed, she asked:

"How is *Fräulein* Sobieski, and why did you come home so early?"

"*Fräulein* wanted to hear all about you and Kyril, and as usual she had lots of gossip to tell me."

Marie-Henriette looked at her enquiringly, and Laetitia said:

"She had heard that Cousin Augustina was determined that Stephanie should marry the King."

Marie-Henriette gave a little laugh.

"*Fräulein* is like Great-Aunt Aspasia—they always know everything about everybody."

Then she said, lowering her voice as if she was afraid of being overheard:

"Have you done anything to help Stephanie? She came here yesterday evening after you had left."

"Not again!" Laetitia groaned. "I warned her that it was dangerous."

"She was frantic because Cousin Augustina had told

her exactly what to say when the King proposed, and
Stephanie was sure there was no longer any hope."

"That is where she is mistaken!" Laetitia said firmly.
"You are not to say one word about it, Hettie, but I am . . .
almost sure . . . in fact I *am* sure . . . that the King will
not . . . propose to Stephanie!"

Marie-Henriette gave a cry of excitement.

"What has happened? What have you done?"

"I cannot tell you yet," Laetitia replied, "because it
might be unlucky. We must just keep praying that the King
will . . ."

She was just about to say: "keep his promise," then she
felt that might involve her in uncomfortable questions as to
whether she had seen him and what they had said to each
other.

Instead she said:

"We must just pray and 'will,' as Papa used to do, that
everything will come right."

"I hope so! I do hope so!" Marie-Henriette said. "At
the same time, I do not believe that Cousin Augustina will
ever allow Stephanie to marry Kyril. She hates us all so
much!"

"I have thought of that," Laetitia replied, "but we
must jump one obstacle at a time, and the first thing we
have to do is to get rid of the King."

As she spoke, she knew it was the last thing, from her
point of view, that she wanted.

She wanted him to be at the Palace so that she might at
least see him or hear his voice.

She knew that even if he did not notice her, if she was
in the same room with him the vibrations between them
that had joined them indivisibly last night would make her
vividly aware of him.

She wondered if perhaps he would feel the same about
her. Then she was quite certain that she was being
presumptuous.

"I feel like this about him because I have known so few
men," she reasoned, "while, according to Great-Aunt Aspasia and *Fräulein* Sobieski, he is surrounded by beautiful,
glamourous women."

It was a depressing thought, and yet it kept on occurring while she was getting dressed.

When she went downstairs she found that her mother had arrived home after having luncheon at the Palace.

Princess Olga was looking very lovely, despite the fact that her gown was three years old, and her bonnet, which she had worn for the same length of time, had been hastily refurbished with some new ribbons.

She had also added a few small feathers from a box in which they kept all the odds and ends which might come in useful.

"Good-morning, my darling!" she said as Laetitia appeared. "Or rather, good-afternoon!"

"I am ashamed at sleeping so late," Laetitia said, kissing her mother.

"It was the best thing you could do. It must have been very tiring riding all the way to the *Fräulein*'s cottage. Was she very ill, as you were afraid she might be?"

Hastily Laetitia remembered that her excuse for going to see her old Governess was that she had sent a message to say that she was ill.

"She is better, Mama, and wanted to hear all about you, and of course Kyril, who has always been her favourite."

The Princess laughed.

"There is no doubt about that!"

Then she said hastily and almost in a whisper:

"She did not know about Kyril and Stephanie?"

Laetitia shook her head.

"No, of course not, but she had heard how unkindly Cousin Augustina treats us all, and that people are very shocked by her behaviour."

The Princess pressed her lips together for a moment. Then she said:

"I have something to tell you which I hope will not upset you."

Then as her daughters looked at her wide-eyed, it flashed through Laetitia's mind that perhaps Cousin Augustina was going to forbid them to go to the Ball.

Slowly the Princess said:

"Augustina has decided that neither of you shall be presented to the King, and she added, rather insultingly, I thought, that you are not to try to attract his notice."

Laetitia gave an exclamation of anger.

"It is not right, Mama, to treat us like that! Surely you objected?"

"I realised that if I did so it would be quite ineffective," Princess Olga replied, "and from the way Cousin Louis looked at me, I was aware that he had already tried to alter his wife's decision and failed."

"I suppose if we had any pride we would not even go to the Ball," Laetitia said.

As she spoke, she knew that however rude the Grand Duchess might be to them, she would go because she wanted to see the King, even if it was at a distance.

She wanted to look at him and be certain that he was as attractive as he had seemed last night, and that the love she felt still surging through her body had not been just the *Voivode*'s magic.

"I am sorry, girls," the Princess said softly.

"You have not told us, Mama," Laetitia remarked, "what you thought of the King."

"I thought him charming!" the Princess replied. "He was not what I expected, and he certainly has the hair and eyes of a Gypsy, which Cousin Augustina has always deprecated. He also has the most beautiful manners and an undoubted sense of humour."

"What made you think that?" Laetitia asked curiously.

"When Cousin Augustina was forcing Stephanie upon him in what I thought was a most embarrassing manner," her mother answered, "there was a twinkle in his eyes, as if he knew exactly what was happening."

She paused before she said:

"I was sorry for the poor child because she was obviously nervous and very apprehensive."

"Of what, Mama?"

"Of being alone with the King," Princess Olga replied. "After luncheon, Cousin Augustina said to him:

" 'I know Your Majesty would like to see the garden,

which I think very beautiful, and Stephanie would love to show it to you.' "

Laetitia drew in her breath.

"Surely that is very unconventional?" Marie-Henriette exclaimed.

"It is certainly something my mother would not have allowed," Princess Olga agreed, "and as if Cousin Louis was shocked, he said firmly:

" 'What a good idea, Augustina! As it is very hot in here, we will all go into the garden.' "

Marie-Henriette clapped her hands.

"That must have annoyed Cousin Augustina."

Laetitia, who had been holding her breath, felt a wave of relief sweep over her.

At the same time, she knew that the Grand Duchess's Prussian obstinacy and determination would not be easily defeated or set on one side.

"She will try again and again," she told herself despairingly.

She wondered if the King, when faced with such a determined schemer, would keep to his promise for the five days decreed by the gods.

Then she remembered he had said that he always kept his promises.

She wanted to trust him and to believe that he would not be easily pressurised into doing something he did not wish to do.

At the same time, Stephanie was very pretty, and if he had to marry someone, his Statesmen and those from Ovenstadt, who had obviously suggested the marriage in the first place, would perhaps prove in the long run more persuasive than the handle of an earthenware jug.

It was the only tangible thing to remind him of the magic they both had seen, heard, and, above all, felt last night.

Because she was so silent, Princess Olga looked at her and asked:

"You are all right, darling? Not too tired after your ride?"

"No . . . I am . . . quite all . . . right," Laetitia answered.

"Well, I think you should both rest this afternoon. Even though you are not allowed to meet the King, I want you to look your best tonight. And there will be plenty of other charming young men at the Ball who will be only too eager to partner you."

Not only because her mother had suggested it, but also because she wanted to be alone, Laetitia lay down on her bed.

She shut her eyes and thought of the King, knowing that her whole life had changed because she had met him and because he had kissed her.

Logically it seemed ridiculous that she should feel as she did after they had met only last night and been alone for only a very short time.

And yet she could not help remembering that her father had said that the very moment he had seen her mother he had known that she was the one woman in his life whom he would ever love, and the only woman he wanted as his wife.

"It was as if a light was shining round her," he had said reflectively. "She looked very beautiful, but it was something more than that: an aura which came from her heart, or perhaps her soul."

"And Mama felt the same about you, Papa," Laetitia said.

"We were very, very fortunate," Prince Paul replied. "We found each other, and after some opposition, by the mercy of God we were able to marry. It is what I pray will happen to you, my dearest, in the future."

When her father had talked like that, Laetitia had thought it was quite possible.

However, now on her bed with the blinds half-drawn to keep out the sun, she knew that even if the King did not marry Stephanie, there was no happy ending as far as she was concerned.

If he found her again, which was very unlikely, or if they met and he wanted to marry her, which really was inconceivable, the Grand Duchess would prevent it.

Feeling as she did about the whole family, she would find it intolerable for one of Prince Paul's daughters to be on the throne of Zvotana.

As a member of the Royal Family of Ovenstadt, Laetitia could not marry without the Grand Duke's permission.

"And Cousin Augustina would never allow him to give me that!" she said aloud. "So, the sooner I erase such ridiculous ideas from my mind, the better!"

That was easier to say than to do, for once again she was feeling that she was in the King's arms and he was kissing her.

She knew that were he a Gypsy instead of a King, she would, if he asked her to do so, follow him wherever he might wander.

'We would be very happy,' she thought with a sigh.

Then, because it was like reaching for the moon and knowing it was completely out of reach, she felt the tears come into her eyes.

* * *

"You both look lovely!" Princess Olga said when her two daughters were ready to set off for the Palace.

Because the Princess had been permitted to be at the luncheon given for the King when he arrived, she had not been invited to the dinner-party tonight, but she would attend the Ball later in the evening.

This, Laetitia learnt, was to consist mostly of neighbouring Royalties, who would stay the night in the Palace or with their relatives or friends who lived nearby.

And of course the Grand Duchess's favourite, the Prime Minister, would also be there.

Although she was not aware of it, there had been another heated argument between the Grand Duke and his wife when he had tried to prevent the Prime Minister from being invited.

"The King will meet all the Civic dignitaries tomorrow when he receives the Freedom of the City," he said firmly, "and I think it a great mistake, Augustina, for him to intrude tonight on what is really a family occasion. The dance we are giving is not only for the King but for Stephanie and young people of her age."

"I want the Prime Minister to be there," the Grand Duchess replied. "After all, it is due to him that the King has come here in the first place, and I think it quite wrong to leave him out of the entertainments we have arranged."

The Grand Duke as usual had been overruled, and although the Prime Minister seemed somewhat out of place, because he was a man of the people and inclined to be aggressive, the Grand Duchess smiled on him approvingly.

However, when she glanced at the King, seated on her right-hand side at dinner, she did not approve of the way in which he was behaving.

Instead of talking to Stephanie, whom she had deliberately placed on his other side, he was talking across her to the Crown Prince of Teck, who had arrived that evening to stay in the Palace.

He was quite a pleasant young man, and the Grand Duchess had at one time thought he might be a suitable match for Stephanie.

Then, just when she was considering a representation to his country, he had become engaged to a Princess from Hungary.

Now she told herself that it would be better still for Stephanie to become Queen of Zvotana, even though there was trouble in the Capital and threats by anarchists upon the King's life.

'He should take a much firmer hand with his subjects,' the Grand Duchess thought to herself.

She determined that once he was engaged to Stephanie, she would tell him exactly how he could enforce discipline upon those who were unruly.

Anarchists were causing a lot of trouble amongst the Crowned Heads of Europe.

There had been attempts on the lives of several of her relations in the North, and King Frederich, whose country lay south of Ovenstadt, had been, just before Christmas, severely wounded by a bomb that had exploded when he was making a speech in his Capital.

'A firm hand is what these people need,' the Grand Duchess thought, 'and a speedy execution for any trouble-maker who is caught.'

She looked again at the King and realised he was talking to the Crown Prince about partridge-shooting, and that Stephanie was not making the slightest effort to join in the conversation.

Instead, she was sitting back in her chair, looking somewhat vacant.

"I shall have to give her a talking to tomorrow morning," the Grand Duchess decided, and turned with a false smile to the Crowned Head on her left.

When they went into the Ball-Room, where a number of their guests had already arrived, the Grand Duchess made it quite clear to the King that he was expected to open the Ball by dancing first with Stephanie.

"I should be delighted," he replied, "but I am sure first there are a number of people who should be presented to me."

As if he was telling her what was her duty, the Grand Duchess stiffened.

"As they have been kind enough to come here to meet me," he went on, "I would not wish them to be disappointed."

There was nothing the Grand Duchess could do but present some of the guests in the Ball-Room, most of whom had a daughter with them, and she hoped they looked as unattractive to the King as they did to her.

A quick glance had shown her that Laetitia and Marie-Henriette were not standing near the door through which the dinner-guests had entered the Ball-Room.

She had made it perfectly clear to Princess Olga that her daughters were not to meet the King.

At the same time, they might push themselves forward, and that would not surprise her.

But she saw that they were effacing themselves in a way with which she could not find fault, although it infuriated her to see them both looking extremely attractive.

Then as the King moved down the room, making no

effort to start the Ball but deliberately talking to any gentleman wearing a large number of decorations, he saw Princess Olga.

She was talking animatedly to the General who commanded Kyril's Regiment.

He had just made some flattering and charming remarks about her son, and she replied:

"What you have said, General, makes me very happy! And now I want you to meet my daughter."

She beckoned to Laetitia as she spoke, and as she came to her mother's side the Princess said:

"Dearest, this is General Leininzen, who has said some very kind things about Kyril."

Laetitia curtseyed, and as the General took her hand he said:

"I might have guessed that you would be as beautiful as your mother!"

Laetitia smiled at him.

"Both my sister and I try to be, but as you can imagine, General, it is a hard task!"

The General laughed.

As he did so, Princess Olga heard a voice beside her say:

"I was expecting to see Your Highness at dinner so that we could continue the conversation we had at luncheon."

"Your Majesty," Princess Olga said, sweeping down into a graceful curtsey.

The King looked at the General, and she said:

"May I, Your Majesty, present General Leininzen, who is in command of my son's Regiment, which was also my husband's."

The King put out his hand.

"I am delighted to meet you, General!"

"I am honoured, Your Majesty," the General replied.

When the King spoke to her mother, Laetitia had thought frantically that she must move away.

Yet, somehow, because he was near her, it was impossible and she felt as if her feet were fastened to the ground.

Then, when she thought she must go, it was too late.

"May I also, Your Majesty, present my daughter Laetitia," her mother was saying.

Laetitia felt herself tremble, and because she dared not look at him, her eye-lashes were dark against her white skin.

But somehow she managed to curtsey.

Then as the King held her hand in his, she felt his vibrations as she had last night reaching out towards her, and she was his captive.

It was as if she were in his arms again and his lips were on hers.

She knew that because he was touching her she was trembling, but still she could not look at him, until as if he forced her to do so she raised her eye-lids and her eyes looked into his.

He was just as handsome and overpowering as he had been last night, and for a moment she was unable to look away.

Then when she was not certain whether he had recognised her or not, the King released her hand and turned to Princess Olga.

"May I have the honour of this dance?" he asked.

For a moment the Princess was too surprised to reply.

Then she glanced a little way up the room to where the Grand Duchess had been caught by an older woman of great distinction, who was holding her in conversation in a way which had made it difficult for her to follow the King.

"I think that would be a mistake, as Your Majesty has not yet opened the Ball," Princess Olga replied.

"In which case, as I am sure everybody is longing to dance," the King said, "I will open it with your daughter!"

He turned to Laetitia as he spoke and put his arm round her waist.

She knew as he drew her into the centre of the floor that she should protest, but her voice had died in her throat.

As the Band, which had been playing rather softly while the King was talking, now burst into the strains of a Viennese Waltz, it was too late to do anything but dance as he wished her to do.

For a moment nothing mattered except that she was close to him again, his hand was holding hers, and his arm encircled her waist.

She saw an expression of fury on the Grand Duchess's face when she realised what was happening, and a faint twinkle of amusement in the Grand Duke's eyes.

There was an expression of relief on Stephanie's face as she looked across the room to where she knew Kyril was watching her.

She did not go to him as she longed to do, she only knew that he was as glad as she was that the King was dancing with somebody else.

For both of them it seemed to be an omen of good luck that things might not be quite as bad as they anticipated.

Not until Laetitia and the King had circled the floor once did the other dancers, according to custom, join them.

Now as they whirled round under the crystal chandeliers, the King said in what seemed to be a conventional tone:

"I am delighted to meet you, Princess. I have heard so much about your father and how popular he was in Ovenstadt."

It was not what Laetitia had expected him to say. At the same time, she was sure he had not recognised her as his Gypsy bride.

"I am honoured, Sir, that you have heard of Papa," she replied. "We all miss him very much, and our lives have never been the . . . same since he . . . died."

"That is what I was told," the King replied.

"By whom? I had no idea that in Zvotana Your Majesty would have heard anything about us or our . . . troubles."

"When I am visiting a country," the King answered, "I make it my business to find out everything I can about its history and its people. In fact, I was told before I arrived how very beautiful Princess Laetitia was!"

He seemed somehow to accentuate her name, and because she was frightened Laetitia missed her step.

"I . . . I am . . . sorry," she said quickly.

"I forgive you," the King replied, "but I want you to tell me a great deal more about yourself. What do you do when you are not dancing at a Ball like this and of course receiving a great number of compliments?"

Laetitia laughed, and because she was now quite convinced that the King did not recognise her, it was a spontaneous sound, before she replied:

"Perhaps you will be surprised, Sir, when I tell you that this is the first Ball I have ever attended, and Your Majesty's compliment is one of the first I have ever received!"

"You can hardly expect me to believe that!" the King remarked.

"It is true, and strangely enough, Sir, I always tell the truth . . . if it is . . . possible."

She spoke without thinking, then realised that she had not been entirely truthful last night, when she had let him think she was with the Kalderash and that she was a dancer.

She felt the colour rise in her cheeks and hoped the King was not aware of it, but she thought that if he was, he would think it was due to the dancing.

They moved round the room again in silence, then as the Band stopped, the King said:

"I will now do my duty, but I must dance with you again, and I insist that you do not leave until I have done so."

He spoke in an authoritative way that made Laetitia stiffen in surprise, then as their eyes met, the Ball-Room disappeared and instead there were only the stars overhead and the *Voivode*'s voice joining them together.

Almost like the crack of a whip was the Grand Duchess's tone as she said:

"I hope Your Majesty has enjoyed the dance, and now you must be gracious enough to dance with your little hostess, who is eagerly looking forward to the honour!"

There was no mistaking the note of acidity behind the Grand Duchess's words, but the King only smiled and said:

"Of course! I shall be delighted, and I believe, Princess Stephanie, that we should have opened the Ball together. You must forgive me if I have omitted to follow one of the customs of your country."

"Oh, no, Your Majesty!" Stephanie said before the

Grand Duchess could prevent her. "It is not a custom of Ovenstadt, but comes from Mama's country, Prussia, and she has introduced it here."

"Then I hope I can be exonerated from making a *faux pas*," the King said lightly.

As the music started again, he and Stephanie began to dance.

Because she had been singled out by the King, and also because there was no doubt that she and Marie-Henriette were the prettiest girls in the room, Laetitia found herself besieged by partners.

Some of them were somewhat old but distinguished, some were young and good-looking, but she knew at a glance that the King was without question the most outstanding man in the room.

It would be impossible for him, even without the glitter of the decorations on his white uniform-coat, not to look far more distinguished than any other man present.

As he passed her on the dance-floor, she could not help wondering if he missed the decoration he had given to the *Voivode* last night and if he had decided that when he returned to his own country he would order another to replace it.

She had found herself wondering several times today why he had given the *Voivode* anything so expensive, instead of the customary gold coins which were part, she knew, of every Gypsy ceremony.

However, it had been a magnanimous as well as a generous gesture and one becoming a King.

She was sure that the *Voivode* would not even think of selling the decoration, but would keep it amongst his other treasures like the gold goblets to be passed down to future generations of the Kalderash.

There was supper halfway through the evening, to which the Grand Duchess made quite certain the King escorted Stephanie.

After midnight the Grand Duke gave the older guests permission to leave because they had some distance to go to their Castles or houses.

The Ball-Room became less crowded, and Laetitia

began to wonder if the King had forgotten the second dance he had demanded of her.

Then, when after the spirited Quadrille she was talking to her partner in one of the open windows of the Ball-Room, unexpectedly the King was beside them.

"The next dance is ours, Princess Laetitia!" he said.

Laetitia did not hesitate.

She had already promised it to somebody else, but she could not refuse the King.

In fact, she had no wish to do so. She longed to be close to him once again because every moment of the evening she had been vividly aware of him. At the same time, she knew it was dangerous.

She was almost certain that he would not recognise her with her dark hair in ringlets on either side of her face and her only ornamentation three white roses at the back of her head.

But there was always the possibility that he would remember her voice, her eyes, or perhaps, and it made her quiver to think about it . . . her lips.

Laetitia's partner bowed to her and said:

"Thank you, Princess, for a delightful dance."

He moved away, and the King, taking Laetitia's hand in his, drew her out through the window and into the garden.

There were just two steps from the marble terrace outside onto the soft grass.

When they reached it, the King without speaking moved away from the lights of the Palace and passed the flower-filled beds and blossoming shrubs until they reached a small fountain in what was known as "the Herb Garden."

Here there were no lights, but there was no need for them.

The stars which had shone above them last night and the moon which had lit the Castle made everything gleam mysteriously silver.

There was a seat just beyond the fountain, and when they reached it the King, still holding Laetitia's hand, drew her down beside him.

Still without saying anything, he pulled from her hand the lace mitten she was wearing instead of white kid gloves.

She did not protest, and she said nothing, for the simple reason that the mere fact that the King was touching her made her quiver with the same excitement he had evoked in her last night.

She also felt, although she tried to suppress it, the fire that had come from his lips sweeping again through her body and burning wildly within her breasts.

When her hand was free, he turned it palm-upwards, and in the moonlight the little mark on her wrist that the *Voivode* had made with his jewelled knife showed dark against the whiteness of her skin.

The King looked at it for a long moment. Then he asked:

"How could you have disappeared in that infuriating manner? How could you have left me when you knew you belonged to me and had become my wife?"

"I . . . I did not . . . think that . . . you recognised me," Laetitia murmured.

The King smiled.

"I was aware that you were somewhere in the room the moment I entered it!"

"How . . . could you . . . know that?"

"Have you forgotten that like you I have Gypsy blood in my veins?" the King asked. "And even if you were not part of the magic which placed us both under a spell, I can still use my intuition and my perception better than ordinary men."

"Did you . . . think last night . . . that I had not gone away with the . . . tribe?"

The King smiled again.

"I was sure of it. In fact, after you had left so unaccountably, I had first to convince myself that you were not an illusion like the bird in the tree or the doves that came from nowhere!"

He gave a little laugh and went on:

"I reasoned it out logically that there must be some good explanation not only for your disappearance but also for your insistence on my fidelity."

He paused, and now looking at him incredulously Laetitia asked:

"Did you . . . really think of that?"

"I am not completely half-witted," the King replied, "and as I have been argued with, pleaded with, and almost compelled to come to Ovenstadt to propose marriage to the Grand Duke's daughter, I can think of only one reason why anybody should try to prevent me from doing so."

"What did you . . . think that . . . reason could be?"

"That the Princess Stephanie does not wish to marry me!"

Laetitia gave a little cry.

"That is clever of you . . . very clever!"

"At the same time," the King went on, "only somebody very close to her could have known her feelings in the matter, and I had in fact heard, even in Zvotana, that Prince Paul's elder daughter was not only exquisitely beautiful but resembled my great-grandmother . . . whose name was Saviya!"

Laetitia clasped her hands together.

"So you . . . knew who I . . . was!"

"Not at first," the King admitted. "I merely thought the gods had been very kind in relieving what would undoubtedly have been a very dull evening in Thor Castle."

The way he spoke made the colour come into Laetitia's cheeks.

"Were you . . . shocked?" she asked in a whisper.

"No, intrigued," the King replied. "But later, with the wine, the magic, and the inexpressible feelings we aroused in each other, I think we both became a little mad, and I knew I must have shocked you! So, you did the only thing you could do in leaving me."

Because it had hurt her and been such agony to do so, Laetitia's hand, which he still held in his, tightened.

As if he understood what she had suffered, the King bent his head and kissed the tiny scar on her wrist.

"Now, Laetitia Saviya," he said, "what are we going to do about us?"

"What . . . do you . . . mean?" Laetitia asked nervously.

"The *Voivode* gave us the magic of love and made you my wife," the King said softly.

"For five days . . . !"

"Or, if we choose, for five years, or fifty-five, or perhaps five centuries."

Laetitia trembled as she asked:

"W-what are you . . . saying?"

"I am saying that you are mine," the King replied, "my wife! Although we may have to be married again to please my people and yours, we are married by the Gypsy laws in which we both believe."

"No . . . no!" Laetitia cried. "It would . . . be impossible!"

"Why should it be impossible?"

"Because I will . . . never be . . . allowed to . . . marry you . . . even if you . . . wanted me to . . . do so."

"*If* I wanted to do so?" the King repeated. "You know what I want without my having to put it into words, Laetitia. We belong to each other."

"It is . . . impossible . . . you cannot be . . . sure!" Laetitia said incoherently.

She looked away from him as she spoke, and the King put out his hand and taking her chin between his fingers turned her face round to his.

"Look at me!" he ordered.

She tried not to obey him, but because he was touching her, and because she felt her whole body vibrating towards him, she could only look up into his face.

Then she felt as if the stars overhead haloed him so that he was enveloped in a strange light that came also from within himself.

She felt her heart leap from her body to join his heart, and the fire which he had aroused within her last night was burning through her again as she knew it was burning in him.

At the same time there was music which rose towards the stars, not from Gypsy violins but from a melody of wonder and glory within themselves.

The King looked at her for a long moment before he said:

"Now tell me the truth—what do you feel about me?"

"I love . . . you!" Laetitia whispered. "I love you . . . desperately . . . but . . . I would not be . . . allowed to marry . . . you."

"How can you be sure of that?"

Because of the sensations that were making her whole body quiver and she could hardly breathe, Laetitia could not find words to explain.

All she wanted to do was to move nearer to the King, to feel his arms round her, his lips on hers, and to know that she need think of nothing and nobody but him.

Then as she stared at him spellbound to the point where her mind seemed to have gone and all she was conscious of was the painful beating of her heart, somebody in the garden laughed.

The sound came from some distance away, but it was as if she were jerked back to reality by a slap on the face.

The King released her, and Laetitia turned away from him.

"You . . . you would not . . . understand," she said dully, "but because the Grand Duchess . . . hates us all, including . . . my mother, she would never . . . allow the Grand Duke to give his . . . permission for us to be . . . married."

"How can you be sure of that?" the King asked again.

"Why do you think we were not invited to the luncheon or the dinner which was given for you? We were also told emphatically that we would not be . . . presented to . . . you at the . . . Ball."

The King frowned.

"It seems incredible, when your father was so popular and was a first cousin of the Grand Duke."

"I know," Laetitia agreed, "but the Grand Duchess is Prussian . . . and she always . . . gets her own . . . way."

"Not with me!" the King said firmly.

"She may not be able to compel you to propose to Stephanie, but she would never in a . . . thousand years allow me to marry you."

"Then we will have to think of a way of circumventing her," the King said, "for I have already given my word as a Gypsy that I will be faithful to you. In any case, I have to be married!"

"Why?" Laetitia asked. "For a . . . Roman Circus?"

The King laughed.

"A very apt description of it, but also, far more important, now that I have met you I not only want to be married but I want my children to be partly Gypsy, as we are."

He smiled before he said softly:

"I hope that they will find the magic that we have found and the love which is more important than anything else in life."

Laetitia turned once again to look at him.

"You . . . really believe . . . that?"

"Do you think I am lying? What does your instinct tell you?"

"That you are . . . speaking the . . . truth."

"Then listen to me," the King said. "It may not be possible while I am here, for I am leaving tomorrow after I have received the Freedom of the City. But somehow, in some way, I shall make you my wife publicly as you are already secretly."

His voice deepened as he finished:

"It may take a little time, but you will have to trust me."

Laetitia drew in her breath.

"If it could . . . really happen . . . it would be the most wonderful . . . perfect thing that could ever happen but I . . . feel it is only a . . . dream."

"Then dream that we will be together as we were last night! Last night when the magic happened, it seemed unreal, and after you had left me, I thought for one incredible moment I had been dreaming, but I knew when I saw you this evening my dream had come true."

The emotional note in his voice seemed to Laetitia like the love-song the Gypsies had played as she and the King had left the plateau to walk back to the Castle together.

The King bent his head and once again kissed the tiny scar on her wrist.

"That shows you belong to me," he said, "and there will be no need in the future, Laetitia, for marks or scars, because our hearts are one. When I kissed you, you gave me not only your lips and your heart but also your soul."

"That is . . . what I . . . felt," Laetitia murmured, "and I knew . . . last night and today when I thought about you that . . . I could never . . . love anybody else . . . or marry . . . another man."

"You are mine!" the King said fiercely. "And I would kill any man who touched you!"

The violence with which he spoke made her feel that it was impossible not to move towards him and not to raise her lips to his.

Then, because there were people near them, the King held himself in an iron control and drew Laetitia to her feet.

"I must take you back to the Ball-Room," he said, "otherwise they will all be talking."

"The Grand Duchess will be . . . very angry!" Laetitia murmured.

"Do not be afraid," the King said. "I know, again with the instinct of a Gypsy, that nothing and nobody in the world can stop us or prevent us from being, as the gods ordained, not two people but one."

He gave a short laugh as he said:

"If you do not trust me, my beautiful one, trust the gods. I can assure you they are very much more powerful than one tiresome, bossy Prussian woman!"

Because the way he spoke was such a contrast to what he had said before, Laetitia found herself laughing.

Then as their feet carried them back towards the lighted windows of the Ball-Room, she knew there was a flame of hope burning irresistibly within her heart.

Chapter Seven

L aetitia went home thinking that the King had taken the stars from the sky to put them in her hands, and it was impossible to think of anything else.

Although when she said good-night to the Grand Duchess and saw the expression of fury in her eyes she knew that she would pay for her happiness when the King had left, it seemed so far away that she was not troubled.

Because their house was so near, they walked back to it through the garden, although, as their mother had said, on such an auspicious occasion they should at least have arrived at the Palace in a carriage.

"As we have no carriage, Mama," Marie-Henriette had remarked, laughing, "that would be rather difficult."

Then there was a little silence while both the girls were thinking that if the Grand Duchess behaved properly, she would send one from the Palace to collect them.

But as they left by the front door, with the servants bowing respectfully, Laetitia was too happy to notice that they were the only guests who had to walk.

But Marie-Henriette, slipping her hand into Princess Olga's, said:

"Now 'Cinderella,' and that applies, Mama, to all three of us, must go back to the kitchen to sit amongst the ashes."

Princess Olga laughed, but it was obviously rather an effort, and only when they were inside their own little house did she say to Laetitia:

127

"I can understand, darling, that you found King Viktor fascinating, but I am afraid we may all suffer because you were so long in the garden with him."

With an effort Laetitia forced herself to listen to what her mother was saying.

"What do you mean, Mama?"

"Cousin Augustina was so angry that she said to me: 'Your daughter is behaving disgracefully, and make no mistake, Olga, I shall take steps to ensure that this sort of thing never happens again.'"

There was silence. Then Marie-Henriette asked:

"Do you mean she is planning to send us away from here or exile us from Ovenstadt?"

"I do not think she will go as far as that," Princess Olga replied, "but she may certainly deprive us of this house, and although I should not tell you so . . . I am frightened."

Because it was so unlike her mother to speak in such a way, Laetitia flung her arms round her.

"Oh, Mama, I am sorry!" she said. "I know I behaved indiscreetly with the King, but it was hard to resist him."

"I can understand that, my dearest," Princess Olga answered. "At the same time, he will go back to Zvotana and forget us, but we are left with Cousin Augustina."

For a moment Laetitia considered telling her mother what the King was planning.

Then, because it meant so much to her personally, and because she did not wish her mother to know how she had first met him, she could not think how she could explain it.

Instead, she said after a moment:

"I do not believe, Mama, that things will be as bad as you anticipate. I have had a very strong feeling lately that Papa is looking after us, and if anybody could stand up to Cousin Augustina, it would be he!"

She knew as she spoke that she had said exactly the right thing.

"You are right, my dear," her mother replied. "Of course Papa will look after us, whatever happens, and it was very feeble of me not to remember that."

"I hate Cousin Augustina!" Marie-Henriette said vio-

lently. "She makes our lives a misery and spoils everything.
I could see she disapproved because that nice young Prince
Ivor of Saxony danced with me three times."

The Princess's attention was diverted from Laetitia.

"I am glad you liked Ivor," she said. "I used to see a lot
of his parents when your father was alive, and they were
both charming."

"I think he will be coming to see . . . me next week,"
Marie-Henriette said.

She blushed as she spoke, then as if she did not wish to
say any more she kissed her mother and Laetitia and ran
from the room.

"Please do not be too worried, Mama," Laetitia
begged. "I have a very strong instinct, which of course
comes from my Gypsy blood, that happiness is waiting for
us all . . . just round the . . . corner."

Her mother laughed.

"You have cheered me up, darling, and I shall think
only of all the nice things that have happened tonight, and
forget Cousin Augustina."

They went up the stairs together, but when Laetitia
went into her own room she wondered if she was perhaps
being optimistic and raising false hopes in her mother as
well as in herself.

Then everything the King had said to her, and the
thrills which had run through her body when he kissed the
scar on her wrist, made her feel once again as if her love
filled the whole world.

She had expected to stay awake worrying, but instead
she awoke still feeling happy, and lay looking at the sun
coming into her room in a golden streak from each side of
the curtains.

Then as she felt the little scar throbbing on her wrist
and remembered the King's lips warm and insistent upon
it, the door swung open and Marie-Henriette rushed into
the room.

"Get up, Laetitia!" she cried. "And hurry! It is so
exciting!"

"What has happened?" Laetitia asked, sitting up in
bed.

"Mama says it is because the King has not proposed to
Stephanie that she is to drive to the Civic Hall in another
carriage with Mama, and we are to go with her!"

Laetitia felt her heart leap with excitement.

The King had not proposed to Stephanie, and now,
although he was leaving today, she would see him again.

It was also unheard of since their father had died for
them to be included in any of the official processions or
Receptions for any visiting dignitaries.

She knew that after being so crushed and ignored, her
mother would enjoy the cheers of the people lining the
route who had not seen her for the last two years.

"Hurry!" Marie-Henriette was saying.

Then she left to run into her own bedroom.

As she washed and started to dress, Laetitia was
thinking hurriedly of what she could wear.

There was very little choice, but because the King
would see her, it was important.

Finally she chose a white gown which she had had for
several years, and which had been expensive and smart
when Princess Olga had bought it for her.

She had altered it and added a row of lace from
another gown to the hem to make it longer, and found as a
sash a pretty chiffon scarf of her mother's which gave it a
dash of colour.

Because it was deep pink it would, she thought
remind the King of her Gypsy skirt and the veil she had
worn over her head when they were married.

Hurriedly, because she knew there was very little
time, she added some deep pink roses of the same colour to
her bonnet, which was at the moment trimmed only with
white ribbons.

Then as she went down the stairs, Gertrude stood
waiting, a cup of coffee in one hand and a hot *croissant* in
the other.

"You're not going out without something to eat, Your
Highness!" she said firmly.

"I ate so much last night," Laetitia answered, "that all
want is a little coffee."

She drank it, and as she did so her mother came down the stairs.

The Princess was wearing a mauve gown which she had bought as half-mourning after wearing black for a year, and which she had never been able to afford to replace.

Because like her daughters she was excited at the thought of driving in the Royal Procession, she looked lovely, and Laetitia said impulsively:

"For once, Mama, you are taking your rightful place at Court, and I expect, if the truth were known, it was Cousin Louis who insisted that Stephanie should drive with you."

"I am sure it was," the Princess replied.

She gave a little sigh as she added:

"Dear Louis said last night how much he enjoyed having all four of us together at the Palace."

"He should take a firmer line with Cousin Augustina to see that it happens more often!" Marie-Henriette said sharply.

Because Laetitia had no wish for her sister to start one of her tirades against the Grand Duchess, she said quickly:

"Come on, let us go to the Palace. If we are too early, we can wait there."

As she spoke she knew that she was really hoping she would have a chance to speak to the King.

Even if they only said "Good-morning!" to each other, she knew their vibrations would be linked together with love, and that to be near him would renew in her the glorious sensations she had known last night.

"Have you got your gloves?" the Princess asked automatically.

Then, as she saw the girls were both carrying white kid gloves, she said:

"You can put them on as we walk across the garden."

Gertrude stood waiting to see them off at the door and remarked:

"I'm real proud of you, and that's the truth!"

"I wish you could come too, Gertrude," Marie-Henriette said.

"Don't you worry," Gertrude replied, "I'll be in the

crowd watching you coming back to the Palace, and nobody's going to stop me from doing that!"

They walked from the courtyard into the garden, and cutting across the drive went over the green lawns, gay with their flower-beds, towards the front door of the Palace.

They were halfway there when they saw an open carriage driving away with an escort of Cavalry in front and behind it.

They all stood still to watch it, knowing that the two people inside the carriage were the Grand Duchess and Prince Otto, on their way to the Civic Hall to be there when King Viktor arrived.

Neither Princess Olga nor her daughters spoke, but they were all thinking the same thing: that it was an insult to the Grand Duke that his wife and son should take his place.

Only when the last horses of the Cavalry were out of sight did the Princess move forward again, and they walked on to the Palace.

As they reached the steps, the sentries presented arms and the Lord Steward stepped forward to bow and say:

"Good-morning, Your Highness. I was instructed to escort you as soon as you arrived to the Salon where His Royal Highness and His Majesty are waiting."

Laetitia felt her heart leap. She would not only see the King again, she would be able to speak to him.

It would take a little while for the Grand Duchess and Otto to reach the Civic Hall to be received by the Lord Mayor and the Prime Minister, so she would have time not only to greet the King but also to talk to him.

The Lord Steward led them to the Salon, and two footmen with powdered wigs opened the doors.

The Grand Duke and the King were alone, and Laetitia guessed that the *Aides-de-Camp* and other people who would accompany them in other carriages were being looked after in another room.

The Grand Duke held out his hand to the Princess, saying:

"Good-morning, my dear Olga! I feel sure you would

like a glass of champagne before we face the crowds and the
ceremony at which inevitably the speeches will be long and
dreary!"

The Princess curtseyed and laughed.

"You must not make His Majesty feel apprehensive of
what is waiting for him, Louis."

She curtseyed to the King, who kissed her hand, and
then Laetitia, having greeted the Grand Duke, was at his
side.

He looked at her in a way which told her without
words how much he loved her.

For a moment she almost forgot to curtsey, then as she
did so and the King's hand touched hers, she felt as if their
love was so strong that it must be impossible for her mother
and the Grand Duke not to perceive it.

Fortunately, at that moment Stephanie came hurrying
into the Salon.

"I am sorry to be late, Papa," she said impulsively,
"but I hated the gown Mama chose for me, so I changed it
as soon as she left!"

She went to her father as she spoke, and put up her
face to kiss him, and the Grand Duke said:

"It seems to me you will be in trouble when your
mother sees what you have done."

"I am always in trouble!" Stephanie replied.

Then as she curtseyed to the King she added:

"I had a tremendous scolding, Your Majesty, this
morning, because you did not open the Ball with me, and I
think it is very unfair that you have got off scot-free!"

The King laughed.

"I am sure because you look so pretty you will
eventually be forgiven."

"I doubt it!" Stephanie replied.

She did not wait for him to answer but kissed Princess
Olga and then the two girls.

They were all aware that she was in high spirits
because the King had not proposed.

Stephanie realised, because she was to travel in another carriage, that her mother had for the moment
accepted defeat.

But that would not mean, Laetitia thought, that the Grand Duchess would give up the chase altogether, or perhaps she had another King in mind.

However, Stephanie's good humour was somehow infectious, and as they sipped their champagne they were all laughing and talking in a way that would have been impossible had the Grand Duchess been with them.

Somehow, although she could not think how it happened, Laetitia found herself at one of the windows with the King a little apart from the others.

In a voice that only she could hear, he said very softly:

"You are even more beautiful than you were last night. Did you dream of me?"

"How . . . could I do . . . anything . . . else?"

It was hard to answer him because little thrills like shafts of sunlight were running through her body, and when she looked into his eyes she felt as if he were kissing her.

"I love you," the King said, "and I swear that if I have to move Heaven and earth to do so, you will belong to me!"

It was impossible to answer, and as she stood looking at him, pouring out her love without words, the door was opened and the Lord Steward entered to say to the Grand Duke:

"I think, Your Royal Highness, it is time that you and His Majesty started for the Civic Hall."

"Of course," the Grand Duke agreed.

He put down his glass and looked round as if he wondered where his distinguished guest had gone, and hastily the King moved from the window towards him.

The two men now walked from the Salon side by side, and Princess Olga and Stephanie followed, with Laetitia and Marie-Henriette behind.

They passed through the Hall where the *Aides-de-Camp* and the occupants of the fourth carriage were, who bowed as they appeared.

The Grand Duke and the King went out onto the steps of the Palace.

There the open carriage which was to drive them to the Civic Hall was waiting.

Ornamented with gold, it was very impressive, and the four horses drawing it had feathered plumes on their heads.

The coachman and the footmen who stood up behind were wearing the crimson, white, and gold livery of the Seventeenth Century with tricorn hats on top of their white wigs.

It was all very grand, and Laetitia hoped that the King was duly impressed, and wondered if Zvotana could equal such splendour.

Then just as the Grand Duke with a gesture of his hand invited the King to enter the carriage first, there was the sound of galloping hoofs, and a moment later an officer on horseback came tearing up the drive.

Because everybody looked in his direction, the King paused.

As he did so, Laetitia realised that the officer who was approaching them at such speed was Kyril.

He drew his horse to a standstill beside the carriage, and as one of the grooms hurried to his horse's head, he walked up the steps to the Grand Duke.

It was not only the speed with which he had ridden but something in his bearing which made everybody wait silently to hear what he had to say.

He saluted the Grand Duke, then surprisingly swept off his helmet before he said very quietly but clearly:

"I regret, Sir, that I bring Your Royal Highness grievous news."

"What is it, Kyril?" the Grand Duke asked apprehensively.

"A bomb has been thrown into the carriage containing Her Royal Highness and Prince Otto! It exploded, and I can only offer my deepest and most sincere sympathy in Your Royal Highness's grievous loss."

For a moment there was absolute silence. Then the Grand Duke asked in a voice that did not sound like his own:

"They are both—dead?"

"There was no chance, Sir, of saving them."

The Grand Duke squared his shoulders. Then he said:

"I must come with you and see what I can do."

"I think that would be a mistake, Sir, if you will forgive my saying so," Kyril replied. "The Doctors are taking to Hospital the bodies of the on-lookers who were killed in the explosion and those who were injured."

He paused and added:

"There is for the moment great confusion and consternation in the city, and therefore it would be best if Your Royal Highness stayed here with His Majesty until things are quieter."

"I understand," the Grand Duke replied.

"I will see to everything, Sir."

Kyril replaced his helmet on his head, saluted, and walking back to his horse mounted it and rode away,

As he did so it seemed as if everybody present was turned to stone. Then Princess Olga moved to the Grand Duke's side to say:

"Kyril is right, Louis dear. There is nothing you can do at the moment, and if the crowds are distressed and panicking, it would be best for you to be here."

"Yes, of course," the Grand Duke agreed.

Forgetting the King, the Princess led the Grand Duke back into the Palace. They walked through the Hall, but instead of going to the Salon they went to the Grand Duke's private room, and the door closed behind them.

As Kyril rode away, Laetitia had taken Stephanie's hand in hers, and now as her father seemed for the moment to have forgotten her, they went into the Salon, followed by the King and Marie-Henriette.

"I . . . I cannot believe . . . it!" Stephanie exclaimed in horror.

"I am sorry, dearest," Laetitia said sympathetically.

"Poor Mama!"

She was not crying, and after a moment the King remarked, as if he was taking charge:

"This has been a tremendous shock and I think we should all have a drink."

He started to pour champagne into some glasses, and as he did so he asked Marie-Henriette:

"Would you like champagne, or would you prefer lemonade?"

"To be honest, I would prefer lemonade," Marie-Henriette replied.

Then as Stephanie and Laetitia sat down on the sofa, she joined the King at the table on which the drinks were laid out and said in a whisper:

"I am not such a hypocrite as to pretend I am sorry!"

"What do you mean?" the King enquired.

"I mean," Marie-Henriette said, "that now there is a very good chance that Stephanie will be allowed to marry my brother, Kyril."

"So that is how the wind blows!" the King remarked, and his eyes were twinkling. "Well, I imagine there can be no difficulties now that he is the Crown Prince."

Marie-Henriette stared at him in astonishment.

"I never thought of that, but of course he is, now that Otto is dead!"

She gave a little sigh that was undoubtedly one of triumph as she said:

"How wonderful! How absolutely wonderful!"

"I should point out," the King said, "that is is not a moment for such elation."

"You would feel the same if you had suffered as we have," Marie-Henriette retorted.

"I have my own reasons for feeling elated," the King remarked, "so I do in fact understand how you are feeling."

Marie-Henriette looked at him speculatively. Then she said:

"Are you telling me that you love Laetitia? You certainly caused a scandal by the way you behaved last night."

"I not only love her," the King replied firmly, "but I intend to marry her!"

Marie-Henriette gave a cry of delight.

"That is the most marvellous, exciting thing I have ever heard!"

She stood on tip-toe and kissed the King's cheek, and Laetitia, looking at them from where she was sitting on the sofa, stared in sheer astonishment.

Marie-Henriette left the King and ran across the room to them.

"Although I know I should not say so, everything is wonderful!" she said. "The King says, Stephanie, that you will have no difficulty now in marrying Kyril, because he will be the Crown Prince, and he is going to marry Laetitia!"

There was a moment's silence. Then as Laetitia began to say: "Really, Hettie . . . !" Stephanie interrupted:

"Is that true?"

"Of course it is!"

"I know that Papa . . . because he loves Kyril, will allow me to . . . marry him."

As she spoke, the door opened and Princess Olga came into the Salon.

Afraid that she might be shocked at anything she had overheard, Stephanie rose to her feet, but the Princess went towards the King.

"I am sorry, Your Majesty," she said, "that we left you as we did. The Grand Duke has asked me to make his apologies and say he was not thinking clearly at the time."

"It was a great shock," the King said quietly, "and although what has happened is deeply regrettable, I can only say how glad I am that the Grand Duke's life has been spared."

"Several people have arrived to see him," the Princess said, "but he has asked me to go back and be with him. He was, however, worrying about Your Majesty."

"I am being very agreeably entertained," the King assured her, "by Princess Stephanie and your daughters."

As if she had almost forgotten her existence, Princess Olga then went to Stephanie, saying:

"I am so sorry, my dearest child!"

"I am quite all right, Cousin Olga," Stephanie replied, "and I know Papa wants you to be with him."

"Yes, I must go back to him," the Princess agreed.

She curtseyed hastily to the King and left the Salon.

Then Stephanie put out her hand towards Marie-Henriette and said:

"Come up to my room with me, Hettie, I want to talk to you."

Laetitia knew, although it might seem heartless, that Stephanie wanted to discuss with Marie-Henriette how soon it might be possible for her to marry Kyril.

It also flashed through her mind that now that the Grand Duchess was dead, the Grand Duke would rely more and more on her mother, and perhaps since they were both lonely people they would find happiness together.

The two girls, giving only very perfunctory curtseys to the King, hurried from the room, and he and Laetitia were left alone.

For a moment they just looked at each other. Then he put out his hand, saying:

"I think we should go into the garden. We might be disturbed here."

She put her hand into his, and thought as she did so that it was impossible to believe that the miracle she had hoped for had become reality, and the flame of hope that had been lighted in her last night would not be extinguished.

They walked in silence through the open window and down into the garden, and she knew they were going to the Herb Garden, where they had sat last night.

It was enclosed by a red brick wall, and now the sunshine on the water thrown upwards by the fountain was creating a million iridescent little rainbows.

In the pool there were some pink water-lilies and a number of gold-fish.

They sat down side by side on the same seat as they had last night, and the King raised both Laetitia's hands to his lips before he said:

"You see, my darling, my instinct was right, and without my having to create a world-stirring revolution, we can be married! But if you think I am going to wait the conventional year of mourning, you are very much mistaken!"

Because she was trembling with excitement at the touch of his lips, Laetitia could only murmur rather weakly:

"Y-you are going . . . too quickly!"

"Nonsense!" the King replied. "I am only emulating your own behaviour, my precious, by going bull-headed at what I want and what I intend to have."

He laughed. Then he said:

"You set me an example of determination, which I can do nothing but admire and follow, and you are hardly the right person to be lecturing me about conventions or propriety!"

Laetitia blushed and took her eyes from his.

"When you talk to me like that," she said a little provocatively, "I begin to wonder if I am the . . . right person to be . . . your wife . . . and a Queen."

"It does not matter whether you are right or wrong," the King replied. "I want you, and I want you quickly."

There was a note in his voice that she had not heard before, and she said:

"I love you, and I suppose I shall do . . . anything you tell me to do, but are you . . . quite sure that you really want me?"

"Can you ask me such an absurd question?" the King enquired.

"I was only thinking," Laetitia said, "that what I did was to save Stephanie from having to . . . marry you, and now that she is safe because the Grand Duchess is dead, you do not . . . have to take a . . . wife from Ovenstadt."

The King laughed, and it was a very tender sound.

"I know exactly what you are doing, my darling," he said, "you are safe-guarding yourself against any reproaches I might make in the future about being pressurised into marriage by you or by magic."

He laughed again before he added:

"But that is exactly what is happening, and you, or Gypsy magic, it does not matter which, have made it utterly impossible for me to marry anybody else. So, the sooner you fulfil your part of the bargain, the better!"

He raised one of her hands to his lips as he went on:

"We are already married according to Gypsy law, which, whether people like it or not, is the law of my blood and yours."

He spoke very seriously, and Laetitia said:

"I love you for believing that . . . and please . . . I want to be your wife, I want it so . . . desperately that it is only because now it is possible that I am giving you a . . . chance to escape."

"I realise that," the King replied, "but there is no escape for you or for me, my darling, now or ever, and I will make sure of that."

As he spoke he put his arms round her and drew her close to him.

"S-somebody . . . may see us!" Laetitia murmured.

His lips were very close to hers.

"Let them!" he said. "The only thing that matters is to convince you for all time that you are completely and absolutely mine."

As he finished speaking his lips were on hers, and as Laetitia felt her whole being melt into his, she knew that what he had said was true.

She was his, and there was no escape for either of them.

* * *

The crowds were cheering madly, their voices rising higher and higher in their excitement!

The sound filled the air deafeningly as the carriage in which the King and Laetitia were driving became filled with the flowers that were being thrown into it.

First the blossoms covered their feet, and now as they were almost waist-high, it was, Laetitia thought irrepressibly, like sitting in a scented bath.

It was impossible to speak, but the King was holding her hand tightly beneath the flowers.

While they waved at the crowds with their other hands, they were conscious only of their happiness and the love which had enveloped them like a blazing light ever since they had been joined as man and wife before the altar in the Cathedral.

It was typical, Laetitia thought, and therefore a portent of the future that the King should have got his way in every particular.

By pretending that the troubles in his country were far

worse than they actually were, he had persuaded the Grand
Duke and Princess Olga that he must not only be married
to Laetitia within three months, but also that their marriage
should take place in his own country.

He had been so eloquent that finally Princess Olga,
then the Grand Duke, raised no more objections.

Therefore, they all arrived to stay in the King's Palace,
finding the elation of the Zvotanians a delightful relief after
the mourning and gloom at home.

Nobody in Ovenstadt, as it happened, was privately
mourning the Grand Duchess, whatever they had to pretend in public, and Princess Aspasia had said frankly to
Laetitia:

"They are longing really to hang out flags because she
is no more! Now everybody can be as happy as they were
before she brought her nasty Prussian ideas into our
country!"

The Grand Duke, however, had to behave in a conventional manner, and while he agreed to allow Stephanie
to marry Kyril, because he was now the Crown Prince, they
were told they must wait at least six months before they
announced their engagement.

"It is not fair!" Stephanie had complained when she
learnt that Laetitia could marry the King so quickly.

"You can see Kyril every day and be with him as much
as you like," Laetitia replied, "but you know that as the
King has so much to do, we can only see each other very
seldom."

It had in fact been almost impossible, because for the
King to arrive in the Capital of Ovenstadt involved a great
deal of pomp and protocol.

Instead, on two occasions, when he said he could not
go on any longer without being with Laetitia, she had, with
Princess Olga, Kyril, and Marie-Henriette, met him at
Thor Castle.

They had stayed there with only the minimum number
of attendants, and Laetitia had managed, because the King
was naturally alloted the best room in the Castle, to be with
him alone in the Sitting-Room where he had first kissed her

and where she had so nearly become his Gypsy wife without the blessing of the Church.

"I love you!" the King said to her the first evening when Princess Olga had allowed them to be together for exactly twenty minutes.

"And I . . . love you!" Laetitia had replied.

"If only I were a Gypsy instead of a King," he continued, "we would not have to do all this damned waiting. We could start off in our caravan, and I could make love to you and tell you how much you mean to me all day and night without half-a-dozen minions knocking on the door and telling me I have another engagement!"

He spoke angrily, and Laetitia laughed.

"It will not be long now," she said, "and, oh, darling, wonderful, magnificent Viktor, I want to be with you just as much as you want to be with me!"

"I do not know what you have done to me," the King said, "or whether it is the magic that the *Voivode* gave us, but I can think of nothing but you."

His lips were on her cheek as he went on:

"While I am passing laws and listening to the most serious debates, all I can see is your face and feel your mouth beneath mine."

It was impossible to answer him because, as if what he had said excited him, he was kissing her.

It was so rapturous and they were so close to each other that she thought it would be impossible for any ceremony in a Cathedral to make them closer.

Now, as they drove on through crowds of people all waving flags, she thought that a new chapter in her life was beginning, and it was so wonderful that there were no words in which to describe it.

When she walked up the aisle on Kyril's arm to where the King was waiting for her, followed by Stephanie and Marie-Henriette as her bride's-maids, she sent up a fervent prayer of thankfulness.

It was not only that it was now possible for her to marry the man she loved, but also that Kyril had taken the place of the spoilt, tiresome Otto, and one day he would be the Grand Duke of Ovenstadt, as she had always wanted her father to be.

She remembered how the *Voivode* had said:

"You must follow your heart."

That was what she had done, and it had brought her everything she had longed for and which she had thought she could never have.

The carriage in which they were travelling had now reached the gates of the City.

As it drew to a standstill and footmen began to clear some of the flowers away so that they could step out, Laetitia saw waiting for them a Phaeton drawn by a superb team of horses.

She knew that was the way they would travel to the King's Summer Palace, where they were to spend the first nights of their honeymoon.

After that she was not certain where they were going, and he had told her it was a secret.

When they had said good-bye to the Civic dignitaries, the King helped her into the Phaeton before climbing into the driving-seat. As he picked up the reins, Laetitia felt once again as if she were in a dream.

Now at last she could be alone with the man she loved, and as they drove off, the King turned to look at her and she knew he was thinking the same thing.

Keeping well behind them was an escort of four troopers of the King's Cavalry, but otherwise they were to be as free as was possible.

"There is no need to be afraid of anything, my darling," the King had said to Laetitia last night. "The authorities have assured me that the man they captured, and who has been executed for the deaths of the Grand Duchess and Prince Otto, was the last real danger in this part of Europe."

"Are you . . . sure?" Laetitia had asked anxiously.

The King shrugged his shoulders.

"Of course there will be others," he said, "but this man had been pursuing me for some time, and was, they tell me now, responsible for the bomb which injured but did not kill King Frederick."

"I shall always worry about you."

"We shall have to ask for a magic spell which will keep us both safe!" the King said with a smile. "But I believe our love is a better protection than anything else, and your beauty will certainly provide my subjects with something better to talk about than the revolutionary ideas which occupied them in the past."

The reports from the Capital confirmed, Laetitia found, that the trouble-makers had all been spurned and ignored because the majority of the populace were interested only in the King's wedding and in seeing his bride.

It delighted her to notice when she was driving to the Cathedral that there were a number of Gypsies amongst those in the crowds waving to them, for, as the King had told her, he had kept his promise.

He had brought in a law that the Gypsies were not to be harassed but were to be welcomed everywhere they went in his country.

"That should bring us luck," she told herself, knowing that the Gypsies of every tribe would give them a very special blessing on their wedding-day.

The King drove quickly and with an expertise that Laetitia had expected, and they reached the Summer Palace in only a little over an hour from the Capital.

It was a white building, set on the side of a large lake and with the mountains of the same range which extended into Ovenstadt rising behind it.

It looked very beautiful in the afternoon sunshine, and as they drew near it Laetitia put her hand on the King's knee to say:

"Our first home . . . together."

"A home, my precious, which we shall fill with the magic of the love which I shall give you tonight."

She blushed at the passion in his voice and the fire in his eyes.

Then as they drove on she said:

"When we arrive, I want you to take me into the garden. I have something very . . . special to . . . show you."

"In the garden?" the King questioned.

"Yes."

He did not ask any more but merely moved his horses on a little quicker, as if he wanted to reach his Palace and have her to himself.

He had given instructions that there were to be only the normal number of servants to greet them when they arrived.

The house was cool after the heat outside, and at first glance Laetitia knew it was very beautiful.

She went upstairs to take off her travelling-cloak and bonnet, and found that her bedroom was more lovely than she could possibly have imagined.

She knew from what the King had told her that it had been redecorated for her.

The blue walls, the pink curtains, and the painted ceiling with cupids rioting amongst gods and goddesses were part of the beauty not only of her dreams but of the bright colours the Gypsies loved.

But she could not wait to look at anything while she was longing to be with the King, and when she ran downstairs, he was waiting for her in a room filled with flowers and with huge windows opening into a rose-garden outside.

He was standing by the window, and as she ran towards him he held out his arms to pull her close to him and kiss her wildly, passionately, demandingly, so that they were both breathless with the wonder of it.

"I thought the day would never come when no-one could ever dispute that you belong to me!" he said. "But now we have been married twice, my darling one, and you are mine as I always meant you to be."

Then, as if he knew that he must control his desire for her a little longer, he said:

"You told me that you wanted to go out into the garden."

"Yes . . . and it is . . . important," Laetitia said. "Do you remember what this is?"

As she spoke she showed the King what she held in her hand.

He looked at it curiously for a moment before he said

"I think it is the bunch of twigs which the *Voivode* had beside him when we were married, but he did not do anything with them."

"It is clever of you to remember," Laetitia said. "He left them for me in the caravan, and I know now why he did so."

"Why?"

"Because, although I never thought it could happen, the *Voivode* knew we were to be . . . man and wife forever!"

In case the King did not understand, she said:

"These twigs come from seven different kinds of trees, and if he had broken them as he would have done in a marriage of the Kalderash, he would have thrown them one by one to the winds."

"And then?" the King asked.

"He would have told us they typified the true meaning of the marriage bond," Laetitia replied, "and it would be impossible for us to break our pledge to each other until one of us had died."

The King smiled.

He took the twigs from Laetitia and snapped them one by one, then threw them amongst the roses in the garden until there were no more.

Then he put his arms round her and said:

"Now I know you believe that we are married forever, not only by the vows that we have just made in Church but by the magic of the Gypsies."

"I knew . . . you would . . . understand."

"I understand, my lovely wife," he said and kissed her.

* * *

Later, they dined in the Dining-Room lit by candles and ate delicious dishes accompanied by a soft, ruby-coloured wine which Laetitia thought tasted very like the wine the Gypsies had given them.

She saw that the King was watching her as she drank, and when she looked at him enquiringly he said:

"You are right, it is the Gypsy wine!"

"How did you come by it?" Laetitia asked.

"Three bottles were left at the Palace yesterday evening," the King replied, "and the servants were told by the Gypsy woman who left them that they were to be given to me personally."

He smiled as he added:

"As you can imagine, the servants were far too afraid of being cursed by the Gypsies if they disobeyed and did not bring the bottles straight to me. There was also a note with them."

"What did it say?" Laetitia asked eagerly.

"It said," the King replied quietly: " 'With the blessings of the Kalderash to a King who has kept his word.' "

Laetitia clapped her hands.

"They were thanking you for making them welcome in Zvotana."

"That is true," the King said, "and when I undid the covering of the bottles, I found there was something for you in the parcel."

"What was that?"

The King drew from his pocket three bracelets.

"These were round the necks of the three bottles."

Laetitia gave a little cry of delight, for each bracelet was fashioned with the exquisite workmanship that she had seen on the gold goblets of the Kalderash.

She knew that not only were they of gold, but the precious stones set in each one were real, one being set with rubies, another with diamonds, and the third with emeralds.

Then as she looked at the three bracelets, she gave an exclamation, and the King said:

"I noticed it too—the colours of the flag of Zvotana!"

Laetitia slipped them over her wrists and said:

"If the Gypsies are grateful, I am ecstatically grateful that, thanks, I am sure, to their magic, I have been able to marry you."

"That is what I thought," the King said, "and now, my darling, because I too am grateful, I have something to show you."

He moved from the table as he spoke, and taking her hand drew her to her surprise not through the door by which they had entered the Dining-Room but out into the garden.

It was a different part from where they had been before, and they walked past shrubs rather than flowers, with trees towering overhead which gave it a feeling of mystery in the fading light.

The sun was sinking in a blaze of glory below the far horizon, and overhead the stars were just coming out, one by one.

It would not be long, Laetitia knew, before it was dark, and the stars would fill the sky as they had the night she had danced round the Gypsy fire and been married by the *Voivode*.

There had been a moon that night, and she knew that tonight there would also be one, which would make them remember the magic and music they had shared together on the plateau below Thor Castle.

The King was not talking but he put his arm round her, and she wondered where they were going until suddenly they came to a little clearing amongst the trees.

It was then that she realised that the trunks were so close together that they seemed almost to form walls round them.

But there was one clear space where they could look over the lake.

It was very lovely with the last rays of the setting sun turning it to gold.

Then when she turned to look at the clearing, she saw on one side of it there were sticks and logs for a fire which had not yet been lit.

On the other side of it was something she had never seen before but which she thought she recognised, even though she was not quite sure.

The King watched her face.

Then as she looked up at him for an explanation, she knew that what she was seeing was a Gypsy bed of flowers such as was always used by the Gypsies after a wedding.

She gave a little gasp, and the King's arms went round her.

"You have bewitched me, my Gypsy wife," he said very softly, "and where else should I make you mine?"

"How could you have thought of anything so . . . wonderful . . . perfect . . . so magical?" she asked.

The King kissed her, then set her on one side.

"First we must light the fire," he said, "then we will drink to our happiness with the wine the Gypsies brought us, and there is one more present I have not yet shown you."

"What is that?" Laetitia asked.

It was difficult to speak or understand completely what the King was saying, because her heart was beating so wildly and she was pulsating with the wonder and rapture he always evoked in her.

Only now it was more intense, more ecstatic than it had ever been before.

The King lit the fire, and as it flared into life and the flames shot up against the darkness of the trees, the sun sank over the horizon and already it was night.

But she could see clearly the cup he held towards her, which was a replica of the "Loving Cup" from which they had drunk at their Gypsy wedding.

It was exquisitely made, the gold engraved with magic signs, the jewels of many colours in it glistening in the firelight.

The King gave it into her hands, then filled it with the wine from the third bottle the Gypsies had brought him.

Then he put his hands one on each of hers, and said in his deep voice:

"This is a 'Loving Cup,' my precious, and as we drink from it I swear I will love you, worship you, protect you, and keep you with me not only all the days of our lives, but for all eternity."

It was a vow which seemed to vibrate on the air, and when he had finished speaking, Laetitia raised the cup to her lips and drank, and the King followed her.

Because the Gypsies had given them five presents and they knew it was a magic number, they each drank five times from the cup.

Then the King set it down on the ground, and as the

flames flared higher and higher, and the stars came out overhead, he drew Laetitia to the blossom-petalled couch.

As she sank down into it, he pulled off his white tunic and threw it down onto the ground before he joined her.

Then as the fragrance in which they were lying seemed to become part of the love she felt for him, Laetitia whispered:

"If this is a dream, then you are my dream-lover whom I have always longed and yearned for . . . but I thought he could . . . never really . . . exist."

"And you are the wife I have been seeking to fill the empty shrine within my heart," the King said, "and I worship and adore you, my darling."

Then his lips were on hers, and as he kissed her she felt his hand touching her body, and something wild and wonderful awoke within her to respond to the passion on his lips.

"I love you, oh darling Viktor . . . I love . . . you," she tried to say.

And far away in the distance she thought she heard the music of the violins.

The King kissed her lips, her neck, then as his mouth moved over the softness of her skin towards her breasts, she knew that the ecstasy rising within them both was part of an inescapable magic.

Then as the flame of the fire leapt higher and higher and there was the scent of the flowers, the wild melody of the music, and the light of the stars, he carried Laetitia up into the sky, where there was only the magic of love for all eternity.

ABOUT THE AUTHOR

BARBARA CARTLAND, the world's most famous romantic novelist, who is also an historian, playwright, lecturer, political speaker and television personality, has now written over 350 books and sold over 350 million books throughout the world.

She has also had many historical works published and has written four autobiographies as well as the biographies of her mother and that of her brother, Ronald Cartland, who was the first Member of Parliament to be killed in World War II. This book has a preface by Sir Winston Churchill and has just been republished with an introduction by Sir Arthur Bryant.

Love at the Helm, a novel written with the help and inspiration of the late Earl Mountbatten of Burma, Uncle of His Royal Highness Prince Philip, is being sold for the Mountbatten Memorial Trust.

In 1978, Miss Cartland sang an Album of Love Songs with the Royal Philharmonic Orchestra.

In 1976, by writing twenty-one books, she broke the world record and has continued for the following six years with 24, 20, 23, 24, 24, and 24. She is in the *Guinness Book of World Records* as the currently top-selling authoress in the world.

She is unique in that she was #1 and #2 in the Dalton List of Bestsellers, and one week had four books in the top twenty.

In private life Barbara Cartland, who is a Dame of the Order of St. John of Jerusalem, Chairman of the St. John Council in Hertfordshire and Deputy President of the St. John Ambulance Brigade, has also fought for better conditions and salaries for midwives and nurses.

Barbara Cartland is deeply interested in vitamin therapy and is President of the British National Association for Health. Her book, *The Magic of Honey*, has sold throughout the world and is translated into many languages.

Her designs, *Decorating with Love*, are being sold all over the USA and the National Home Fashions League made her "Woman of Achievement" in 1981.

Barbara Cartland Romances (book of cartoons) has just been published and seventy-five newspapers in the United States and several countries in Europe carry the strip cartoons of her novels.

Barbara Cartland's
Library of Love

**The World's Great Stories of Romance Specially Abridged
by Barbara Cartland For Today's Readers.**

☐ 20935   **LOVE'S HOUR by Elinor Glyn**   **$2.50**

☐ 20500   **LOVE IN A MIST by Pamela Wynne**   **$2.50**

Barbara Cartland

The world's bestselling author of romantic fiction. Her stories are always captivating tales of intrigue, adventure and love.

☐ 23285	GYPSY MAGIC #173	$2.25
☐ 23284	THE UNWANTED WEDDING #172	$2.25
☐ 23194	LOVE AND LUCIA #171	$2.25
☐ 23192	JOURNEY TO A STAR #170	$2.25
☐ 23191	A KING IN LOVE #169	$2.25
☐ 23245	THE DUKE COMES HOME #168	$2.25
☐ 23162	LOVE ON THE WIND #167	$2.25
☐ 23161	FROM HATE TO LOVE #166	$2.25
☐ 22918	A MARRIAGE MADE IN HEAVEN #165	$2.25
☐ 22876	MISSION TO MONTE CARLO #161	$2.25
☐ 22822	WISH FOR LOVE #160	$2.25
☐ 20574	LOOKING FOR LOVE #152	$1.95
☐ 20505	SECRET HARBOUR #151	$1.95
☐ 20235	LOVE WINS #150	$1.95
☐ 20234	SHAFT OF SUNLIGHT #149	$1.95
☐ 20126	AN INNOCENT IN RUSSIA #148	$1.95
☐ 20014	GIFT OF THE GODS #147	$1.95
☐ 20013	RIVER OF LOVE #146	$1.95
☐ 14922	A PORTRAIT OF LOVE #145	$1.95

Buy them at your local bookstore or use this handy coupon for ordering: